Heroes of Asgard: Book of Verdandi

Book 2 of Odin's Sacred Runes

Nathan Anderson

Edited by: Diana Kupke

Book cover artwork: DC Wince

Copyright © 2022 Nathan Anderson

All rights reserved.

ISBN: 9798353825203

DEDICATION

I'd like to dedicate this book to the men that raised me. My father, and my uncles that taught me about fatherhood while I was young. The friends that were there and those that were not. You helped me understand the meaning of kinship. The teachers that guided me to discover answers instead of throwing facts hoping they stuck. Respect without judgement is the honour unseen. I'm grateful to you all that have been part of my team.

CONTENTS

	Acknowledgments	i	17	The Nutcracker	78
1	Introduction	8	18	Responsibility vs Intelligence	86
2	Gift of Verdandi	10	19	Beware the Krampus	91
3	Peace, Love and Joy	12	20	A Gift Under the Tree	96
4	Sleigh-pnir	18	21	He Sees You When You're Sleeping	99
5	Cupid	26	22	Reindeer Games	103
6	Yule Goats	30	23	He Knows When You're Awake	109
7	The Elven Workshops	36	24	It's the Season for Love and Understanding	112
8	Manufacturing the Gifts	40	25	Children Playing and Having Fun	117
9	Blitzen	45	26	Fishing for a Great Gift	122
10	One Horse Open Sleigh	49	27	Time for Celebration	126
11	The Grinch	54	28	Three Wise Men	130
12	Thor's Wedding	59	29	Away in a Manger	135
13	Seasons' Greetings	63	30	Tanzanite	139
14	Ignorance vs Innocence	69	31	Written in the Stars	144
15	Yule Tidings	73		About the Author	150

ACKNOWLEDGMENTS

Padraic Colum and PogányW. (2019). *The children of Odin : the book of northern myths.* New York, N.Y.: Aladdin

Snorri Sturluson and Arthur Gilchrist Brodeur (2010). *The prose edda : tales from Norse mythology.*

Larrington, C. (2019). *Poetic Edda.* Oxford University Press.

Saxo, G. and Hansen, W.F. (1983). *Saxo Grammaticus & the life of Hamlet : a translation, history, and commentary.* Lincoln: University Of Nebraska Press.

Reaves, W.P. (2018). *Odin's Wife.* Amazon: KDP self-publishing, p.363

Introduction

In Odin's Story: Book of Urd, I told you my background and my theories, but the purpose of this book was to expand the tales. I wanted to show that despite the vastness of the world, it is connected through ancient stories. All these connections may be divided by tongue but somehow their descriptions showed similarities.

The tales and myths, when pieced together, were linked like a rough jigsaw but it wasn't my only intention for this story. I wanted to connect fantasy to reality. I desired to fall in love with travelling again. Even when the world was closed, your mind can travel. Memories and wonders fill the lands we inhabit. Literal landmarks and wonders of the world that even have the most intellectual minds wondering "how?"

The gods were never one-dimensional characters in my opinion. Their stories and links to things seemed to evolve. Someone is not born a warrior or hero. It is their choices and wisdom that manifest. Character is developed through choice and experience. Circumstances are not always within our control but our response to them is the only freedom we have. It is our choice of how to act in times of success and struggle that develops our character.

The gods in my opinion are the same. They evolve and rise to each challenge they face as they develop their inspiring characters. Thor is a heroic god of battle but becomes linked to family life and agriculture with his wife, Sif. Tyr was a brave levelheaded war god but shrank into the background. Freya evolves into Frigg and Loki devolves into madness.

At first, the stories showed a close bond between Odin and Loki. Eventually, Loki's allegiance wavered from Asgard for a bunch of unknown reasons. His character evolved which showed that there was more than what was being shown in the fragmented pieces of the Eddas. It reminded me of an old saying. "Keep your friends close but keep your enemies closer." Was the blood oath with Odin a mistake or did Odin know more?

Odin's story had to be written to deliver the Havamal entertainingly. I wanted to write Heroes of Asgard to show that nothing is born a certain way. It grows into what it becomes due to a variety of different factors. Time has a way of teaching us more about ourselves than any teacher. Although the gods seem to live longer than us, they too might learn a few things along their journeys.

Gift from Verdandi

Greetings, excellent host, It would appear our paths have crossed once more. May I sit again? Much has happened since we spoke last. How should I start this tale?

Well, in the past, the world was less complicated. The realms became lands and no longer have borders. However, the veil between the living and the dead remains strong. The Jotun now live amongst humans, in disguise. Most stay in human form in peace but now and then, you hear stories. Strange sounds in the distance. People go missing in forests, at sea or in mountainous landscapes.

The elves and dark elves are just as volatile. At times, you can feel the presence of a type of dark elf taunting you, causing you fortune or hardship on a cold winter's night. Sometimes, you can even sense the elven spirits in an animal companion. The world is full of awe but only to those that have the imagination to wonder. When you walk through nature, when you take in the beautiful landscape, you absorb its effects on how you feel.

Verdandi can be a gift, or a curse, depending on how you, yourself, respond to the challenges she presents to you. The way someone carries themselves in the face of fears, dangers, failures and victories will determine one's honour in life. It will always be better for a person to act rather than react. Verdandi presents challenges for us all. Whether it be the loss of a loved one or winning the lottery, she gives us the gift of how others perceive us. That is a great gift indeed. You are creating the perceptual view of others' opinions of your character. How would you like others to see you?

When challenged by a troll on the internet, an ogre at the bar, or a giant dragon of a boss, logic will always be your best weapon. Their perceptual reality will be different from your own. No one goes to war thinking, "we are the bad guys." Does chaos need more chaos to become controlled? Well, that's up to you, my good host.

These stories I'm about to tell will take you on a journey and show how a leader has to appear in various situations. Sometimes you must act dumb to allow others to feel important. Other times you appear weak to enable others to feel strong. And leaving to enable others to be present. The main point is always to keep control.

It is ok to wear many hats in life. A mysterious blue hood, a grey wide-brimmed hat, or a red one with fluffy white trim all have their roles. But be cautious about keeping those that wear many faces. They will always be concerned about appearing greater than others. Foolish they are as no one is better than another. Even a god's character is created from their individual experiences in life.

Peace, Love and Joy

It was a cold winter season in Asgard. Snowflakes fell by the billions, and the chill was so bitter it took hold of your very bones. Thor was protecting Midgard, defeating giants. It had come to my attention that our little village was unprotected. If a considerable Jotun force decided to attack, we would lose our homes. The Jotuns would destroy our position as rulers of the realms and chaos would ensue. I summoned a gathering of gods by the fireside to discuss our next move. The skies beautifully glowed red as the flames danced, illuminating the world. It was a sign to those in Midgard that the gods were discussing action.

Freya was first to arrive with Freyr. He went by Lord Cernunnos by the elves he governed, but we would call him Freyr in Asgard. Njord followed soon after with Sumarbrandr in its sheath. "I was bored in Nóatún. Not many boats sailing in the winter, Odin," Njord informed me.

"Probably wise, dear friend, the waters hold more dangers in the icy months."

Tyr came in soon after. "Where is my little brother Thor?" he asked.

"He's off to the lands of Ireland. Two giants are causing trouble for the mortals. They are building a causeway," I replied.

Heimdall was next, travelling from Himinbjörg. Loki and Sif attended last and now the discussions could begin for Asgard's protection.

"Now we can discuss what to do next," I said.

"Ah yes, without Thor, we are left vulnerable, my good king," Sif said gracefully. Her voice was so beautiful that it could enchant the crops to grow each year.

"Sssooo the great Odin is scared his mighty son isn't here to fight his battlessss?" Loki smirked.

"You should show some respect, fool. Odin is our leader," Sif snapped back.

"Thank you, my dear Sif, but Loki knows his place is only temporary on the council. His sly remarks are how he tries to prove his worth by dismissing everything else," I said, bringing Loki's fork tongue to a halt. "Now, with the absence of Thor, we need to discuss Asgard's security. Thor is our mighty defender, but I fear in his absence, the Jotun or Verdandi will try to attack," I announced to the council.

Njörd stepped forward, "with my blade. I can slay anyone who dares to cross swords!".

"A great king you are and a good weapon you have, but what about the days you spend at Nóatán? Asgard would be left defenceless again," I replied.

Freya tossed a log on the fire. "Perhaps we need to build our defences. Walls that are taller than any giant. A barricade so impenetrable that no Landvaetr can fly through gaps."

"Would the great dwarves of Svartalfheim be able to construct such a task?" I asked.

"No, Odin! With your influence on Fafnir and Regin, not to mention Fjalar and Galar. The dwarves will not build your wall. To even suggest it would provoke a war," she warned.

We continued our discussions long into the cold night while someone watched from Mimir's well. Deep in the heart of Jotunheim. A sinister glow came from Mimir's cave. The shadowy figure used my eye and the power of the well to spy and plot the destruction of Asgard. "Ah, poor Odin. Left defenceless without your mighty stag to protect you. That gives me an idea," the witch plotted while cackling at her devious plans.

The following day, the embers of the fire dimmed. The clouds thickened in Midgard from the light smoke that drifted lightly throughout the sky lands. Over the Bifrost, someone approached. It wasn't normal to have visitors as last time was Verdandi under the name of Gulveig. Asgard's visitor was mysterious with his hood and his magnificent horse.

The horse was a large breed, with a beautiful white coat that shimmered like the white snow in the sunlight. The magical stallion had a long and sharp horn on its forehead like a sword pointed toward its enemy. "Such a beautiful horse, stranger. How may we assist you in your travels?" I politely asked.

"Well, wise one, word spreads through the nine realms quickly. You require something," the stranger murmured under his hooded cloak. Using my all-seeing eye, I could identify the shroud of magic surrounding the horse and man.

"It would appear so," I replied suspiciously. I knew Verdandi had sent him. I just wasn't sure of his true identity.

"I am the greatest builder in all the lands. I have built Thrymir's keep. I constructed the great wall of Midgard. Even the Pyramids were easy for me to make," the hooded traveller proclaimed.

"You certainly are qualified for the task we require, but what is the price?" I asked as the bartering began. The hooded man shuffled his feet at least, trying to appear a fool as he thought of the price he had already determined with the one who sent him.

"State your price, stranger!" I exclaimed tiredly of the false pretences.

"Well, wise one, I would like the joy of the sun, the comfort of the moon and the love of a good woman," he declared proudly.

"The first two I've granted to every being in the lands. The last is not mine to give good builder. Love is the prize we all desire but must earn on our own. Love requires patience, understanding and support for a mutually beneficial future."

"No, Allfather, you misunderstood my request. I will build your high impenetrable walls, and while you remain behind them, I will take your happiness, your comfort and the one you love, your Freya," he smirked beneath the cover of his dark hood.

The price was too high to agree, but it was not for me to decide. Freya was my lady, but she was also her own. It would be her choice and her decision in the end. Love is not ownership but an agreement that each would remain trustworthy, honest and above all, help each other when they could.

I retired back to Valhöll to discuss the terms of our defences. Freya's cats cowered beneath the table as the ground began to shake. She was furious, and rightly so. She is my love, and protection from others doesn't gain it for another. We called for Sol and Mani to join the council as they were also on the table for bargaining.

The discussions became heated between the gods at the fire. Outrage at the price demanded because others can give you protection, but they deserve only your respect, not your reasons for living.

"Lisssten brothersss and sistersss, what if we did accept his termsss but added our own," Loki suggested cautiously. The room fell to silence as all turned and glared at him. The ground began to rumble, and Sol's and Mani's glow dimmed. "Hear me out, hear me out," Loki said, trying to ease the tension in the hall. "three of our conditions will prove the task impossible to complete. He must complete the task on his own. He must complete the work at high standards, and he must complete it in three seasons.".

I kept quiet to let the other gods make their own decisions. Most agreed because, logically, it was a great plan. My Freya's ground-shaking temper eased. She knew as much as I, if not more. "If so much as one weakness is left in the wall, the wager is off," my lady declared.

"Yesss yesss, of course, mother," Loki reassured.

The other gods weighed the decision, and all agreed. They looked to me for confirmation, but I looked blankly at them. "Loki, this is your chance to prove your worth. I need your oath that Freya will remain in Asgard and the noble Mani and Sol will return to their duties. Swear it, oath brother!" I exclaimed.

"I ssswear it, Odin."

Loki approached the hooded stranger standing next to his magnificent horse. As Loki gazed upon the beast, he recalled encountering the dwarven warrior he cursed. The unicorn appeared startled and began to rear at him. Loki glared at the horse. "Nice to see you again, Andalfari," he said sinisterly on his approach.

"No, this great horse is called Svadilfari. It is the hardest and best working horse in all the realms," the hooded man proclaimed.

"Ah, I knew him in another life. But that's a long story. I'm here to discuss your terms, great wall builder.".

The builder grunted and coughed while he shuffled his feet.

"Three years, a wall tall enough to make Ymir watch his step if we weren't floating amongst his brains. A wall that is so perfect that no Landvaetr can slip through. Those are my terms," the hooded builder said.

"We have our conditionsss before we can agree to the price," Loki replied.

"I figured you would," the builder snarled.

"You are to complete the work alone."

"You wouldn't grudge me help from my steed, would you?"

"No, that'll be fine. The second condition is you have three seasons, not three years," Loki smirked. The hooded man started pacing with concern. "And the third is perfection. If a single imperfection is found by the deadline, you will receive nothing." Loki's smirk grew to a grin.

The man's pacing quickened. The cold icy air was almost as harsh as the conditions presented. Loki thought the builder would be a fool to accept, but if he did, there was no way the gods could lose. As the man's pacing slowed, he turned towards Loki. The panic fell from his face. As his hood lifted, revealing his expression. Loki saw a smile that sent a shiver up his spine.

"Deal," the builder said before spitting in his hand and sealing the terms with a handshake.

Sleigh-pnir

The terms were set, and the next day the builder sent his unicorn for raw materials. The builder moved with haste; he began to dig quicker than anyone or anything I've seen in all my years. Such an unnaturally powerful being that was stronger and faster than any human, Jotun or Landvaetr. The magic aura that only I and another could see hinted more to what was presented to us.

Leaving the builder to his work, I returned to Hlidskjalf to view the beautiful majestic horse. The sunlight glistened in its white coat and the horn gleamed. There were four quick steps followed by a leap. It galloped hard toward the mountains with a strange contraption towed behind. Watching in awe, I could see its horn cutting the stone and watched as the rock rolled into the sleigh.

The sleigh was magnificent, carved and engraved with runes from the sturdiest elm trees. It could slide across land, sea and air if pulled quickly enough. It glided above the thick snow and kept control over slippery ice. It was far more diverse than a wagon, and it seemed to be specifically designed to carry heavy loads at an incredible pace.

Days turned to weeks while the builder prepared the foundation for Asgard's wall. He scraped and shoveled dirt into high mounds around the perimeter with ease, barely breaking a sweat. It was remarkable for someone so small to complete an impossible task and at an exponential rate.

"Loki, what do you see?" I asked in an attempt to teach him.

"A builder that is working at a rapid pace. But it is early, and the seasons have yet to take hold, and fatigue will set in. Relax, Allfather. He cannot complete hisss tasks," Loki reassured.

I turned to Freya, and she nodded in confirmation. "What do you know, Loki?" I quizzed further.

"The horse and I have history. When I gained the treasure for Hreidmar, I cursed the mighty dwarf Andalfari to his current form," Loki informed me.

"A magnificent steed, powerful and majestic, would be an excellent horse for any king," I mentioned while returning to view the builder and his incredible feats.

It was nearing the end of the first season, and the foundations were completed. Svadilfari, the unicorn, had been stockpiling rock and stone from mountains far away near the builder.

"Three months have passed, Loki. His pace hasn't slowed, and with his steed's help, he will surely finish his task," Tyr expressed concern.

"You better not lose our mother, Loki," Freyr threatened.

"Thisss will be fine. Ssstop worrying, my fellow godsss.".

"What do you see, Loki?" I asked again.

"I sssee him completing his tasssk and me breaking my oath, Allfather," he said, wallowing in shame.

"What do you know, Loki?" I probed further.

"Without hisss horse, he will fail," he sinisterly grinned.

"I'd like that horse, Loki. Do not treat it the same as Otter Hreidmarson," I warned him.

"Yesss Odin, if my plan works, I'll ensure you will have all you desssire," Loki slyly reassured. He left Valhöll to concoct his devious plan.

The builder threw stone after stone in quick succession. They were perfectly placed like puzzle pieces. It was awe-inspiring. Flawlessly smooth and intimidatingly tall, the perimeter would be the perfect defence against the outer realms. However, I was not willing to give up my lady or the life of those mortals in Midgard. I looked towards Freya for reassurance, but she remained confident, returning my look of concern with a comforting smile. It eased my trouble, but I still looked on curiously.

The last season of the wager began as the snow and ice returned. The pace of the hooded builder never slowed, not even for a moment. His mastery over his craft was enchanting as everyone looked on with concern.

"We are going to lose her," Freyr stated.

"Why are you not concerned, lady of the Vanir?" Tyr asked curiously.

"Loki will keep his oath. I know it," Freya eased Tyr's mind.

I turned my gaze toward Svadilfari in the distance. He heaved the sleigh full of everything needed to complete the builder's challenge. The mighty steed pulled through wintery blizzards and up steep landscapes. The sleigh slid over all terrain with the powerful unicorn drawing it.

At the mountain base by the water's edge, another horse appeared. It was a beautiful mare with a coat so white it shimmered in the moonlight. It trotted most gracefully in the snow, appearing and disappearing like a mirage as the snowflakes floated to the ground. Svadilfari looked up, pausing for a moment. The unicorn's heart raced as the attractive appearance enchanted him to lose all awareness of his task. Svadilfari's jaw dropped slightly as his eyes widened. The pretty mare walked into the water seductively, gently splashing in the lake. Svadilfari began to prance as his heart quickened. He was a victim of another's beauty, which happens often. Steadily moving closer to the water, he neighs for the horse's attention.

The unicorn pursued the white mare prancing into the shallow water. Further, it went until the shallows became deeper with every step. Odd though, the beautiful white mare made the body of water appear like a puddle. The water was only up to her ankles, but ignorant to the danger presented, Svadilfari waded deeper. Before long, the cold dark water was up to his belly, and the mare was only just out of reach. The horse's beauty hypnotised, Svadilfari to ignore all caution. Now there were only the eyes, nostrils and mouth above the surface. With one mighty leap, the magnificent unicorn mounted the mare's back.

Suddenly, the mare's beautiful white glow faded to grey. The mare's eyes became the darkest of black. Those monstrous mirrors reflected Svadilfari's horror when he realised all wasn't as it appeared. He tried to scramble off the twisted creature's back, but he was stuck. The harder he struggled, the more hope for survival was gone. He pushed himself up but the grey coat became sticky like black tar. Each time he reared up the tar pulled him tighter on the Kelpie's back.

The beast had a look of death in its eyes that would devour the courage of any brave soul. It began swimming deeper underwater leaving the noble unicorn gasping for air. The deeper it got, the darker it was. As black as the murky waters, you could barely make out its form. The creature became a reflection of its true nature. What once appeared beautiful was twisted and misshapen. The nightmarish thing turned back toward Svadilfari as he was trapped on its back like a fly in a web. The struggle intensified, causing currents beneath the surface of the water. With a turn of its head, the beast bit down on the horn, snapping it clean off. Svadilfari's screamed with agony and pain until his life was no more. Only a few bubbles which popped on the surface could be seen, but I saw deeper. I could see the unicorn's undignified end.

Meanwhile, the builder placed the last stone from his stockpile. "Where is that horse of mine?" he pondered. "Freya, better send for Sol and Mani because you are coming with me!" he shouted toward my lady.

Such ignorance, sure his ability to construct perfect walls was there, but his victory is not reliant on his talent alone.

"Can you gods see my great horse? It should have been back now," the builder asked with a slight degree of concern.

"He has become a victim of foolishness, dear builder. An age-old tale that not all things of beautiful appearance share the same nature. Being enchanted by one's aesthetics and ignorant to the possibility of danger will leave you drowning in your misery," I informed.

"My horse is dead?" the builder asked as his worry grew. "Now, I'll never complete your wall, and Verdandi will not be pleased," the builder mumbled.

The builder became agitated. His fists clenched as his knuckles whitened. He paced back and forth quickly. Sol and Mani landed nearby to watch the outcome of the wager. Njord appeared to be taken by Sol's beauty, but another also desired her. Suddenly, the builder threw his hooded cloak off. As it drifted on the breeze to the floor, something began to happen—a horror from the deepest and darkest of imaginations. The builder twisted and cracked. Teeth were replaced with tusks. His very bones groaned as his size expanded. A hundred times the size he once was, all became clear. The mortal man was a mountain giant from Jotunheim.

"Damn gods! Maybe I'll take my prize. What can you do to stop me without your little Thor?" he grunted and bent down to collect Sol and Mani.

"Release them, giant! I will win Sol's hand after I slay you with the mighty Sumarbrandr!" Njord declared.

"That weapon has an impressive legend. But not in your hand, little king of the Vanir," the Jotun replied, grinning at the challenge. Both squared up against each other, standing toe to toe.

"Perhaps I'll write my legend with the blade using your blood, monster!" Njord threatened while his hand gripped firmly on the sword's handle. Before he could have a chance to unsheath his weapon, the giant attacked. One kick sent the king of Vanaheim flying, only stopped by the impact of Asgard's mighty walls.

After seeing his father defeated, something stirred in the king of Alfheim. He grabbed his elven helmet. It was as green as pine leaves—Evergreen, unaffected by the harshness of winter or the blistering heat of summer. That is probably why the Celts called him the Greenman. It had two antlers on either side of the helm that made him appear deer-like in the shadows of the forests of Alfheim.

"Let Sol and her brother go," Freyr said as he walked up to the mountain giant.

The giant laughed mockingly. Chuckles became huge booming laughs. "You don't even have a weapon. What can you do?"

Freyr looked back at his father's unconscious body, and then he looked into Sol's eyes. His heart raced as he strolled toward the laughing giant. Just like before, the giant kicked, but this time, he missed. The smile on the giant's face was replaced with anger. He swiped and swatted at Freyr, but each time he'd miss, and it only fuelled the giant's rage.

"All those years building great structures, you stood by and watched me claim lives in the thousands. Why?" the builder puffed.

Freyr danced from strike to strike. It was elegant. As the giant began to tire, Freyr smiled. "The purpose of gods is not to accomplish things for others, giant. It is to inspire others to accomplish greatness for themselves," Freyr said in between attempted blows.

The giant swatted more rapidly. His breath became heavier as his every blow's strength weakened. Freyr grabbed an antler from his helmet and ran up the giant's leg to his knee. He leapt from the giant's knee, plunging the antler deep into the giant's heart.

Sol and Mani thanked the young king for their rescue.

"May I take your hand, Sol?" Freyr asked.

"No king of elves. I am promised to another," she replied regretfully.

"Perhaps you have earned a weapon for your feats, noble Freyr. The great Sumarbrandr your father attempted to wield. What say you, king Njord?" I asked as he regained his consciousness.

"Ah, ok, my son's protection of his mother, the beautiful Sol and the noble Mani has earned him the great sword," Njord said, proud of his boy's accomplishments.

"Since you saved us from that horrible giant, perhaps we can give the sword more power," suggested Mani. Sol and Mani waved their arms, spoke magical incantations, and blessed the sword.

Sumarbrandr was granted the power of summer. It gave Freyr the ability to grow crops for the summer's harvest. Freyr bent down to retrieve his antler from the giant's chest before sheathing his blade and returning to Valhöll.

Sol and Mani returned to their chariots and duties in the sky, ensuring Verdandi's wolves did not claim their prey and start Ragnarok.

Nine days later, Loki returned. He looked sheepish but he wasn't alone. A haunting vision behind him. It was a creature that would give children nightmares. It was somewhat familiar but not what I had desired. It was a horse, yes but also not. It was uniquely beautiful, but like most things of beauty, it had its dangers. "Behold, Svadilfari, Odin," Loki declared.

"What have you done, Loki?" I asked. Before he could answer the question, my eye saw the truth.

"Once a beautiful, elegant unicorn, but now an eight-legged Kelpie. A horse that can travel over land and water with great haste. How do you suppose Odin rides on it without it dragging him deeper into the water to join Hel at her table?" Thor asked as he barged through the doors.

Loki lowered his head, pulling the contraption that Svadilfari used to pull mountains from their roots.

"Behold Sleipnir, the sliding one! May it allow Odin the ability to glide over land, water and air! And may it give him the power to slide between the veil of life and death," Loki said to everyone in the hall.

"Thank you, Loki. Today you gift me three things by fulfilling your oath—Asgard's defence against threats from Jotunheim. A noble horse that is quicker than any other, and a chariot, unlike any other. Sleipnir the sleigh!" I declared to the rest of the gods.

As the gods departed, Thor congratulated Freyr on his victory. Loud boasts and thunderous claps celebrate Alfheim's lord Cernunnos. Loki kept to the shadows and hid among the crowds of elves and gods, in fear of judgement and mockery about his actions with Svadilfari.

Cupid

Cupid, in Greek myth, is a child of love and war. He seeks love for others which usually backfires on him and the person leaving them victims of lust. Lust is a fool's game, good host. If you base your love on superficial reasons, your heart will be doomed when things change. Change is inevitable. It shouldn't be feared or mourned. It should be embraced because love is deeper than what appears on the surface.

Well, this tale begins when Loki borrowed the cloak I gave his mother so a long time ago. He soared above the skies, drifting on the breeze and gently gliding above the lands below. He searched and scanned for any sign of the one he had mistreated before, the mother of monsters called Verdandi. He had a dark history with her, and he wasn't finished. He desired to create more monstrous creatures with her from the deepest and darkest corners of his twisted mind.

He flapped and fluttered his falcon feathers between blissful moments of serenity, soaring through calm clouds. He relished the freedom of the skies, almost intoxicated with its power. He flew over Midgard, over Svartalfheim and higher above Jotunheim. He scanned and scoured the forests and mountains, looking for the one that could fulfill his desires.

Loki flew on the wings of love until he laid his falcon eyes on Thrym's keep. It was high in the mountains, concealed by a thick fog. He drifted down closer, curious to inspect the gigantic and intimidating castle. He perched high up on the window's ledge, quietly looking on as the Jotun feasted.

Every type of Jotun gathered in the hall: the sasquatch, trolls, the Yowie, and even the Yeti. Scanning the hall, he quietly searched for the one he burned so long ago. Remaining unnoticed, he realised this gathering of Jotun would be a considerable threat to Asgard. Still consumed by

Loki's lustful desire for more power, he continued observing for a hint of Verdandi's location.

Suddenly, an imposing figure entered the room. It was a Jotun far more significant and more imposing than the rest. Almost all those in his hall raised from their seats and cheered his entry. "HAIL KING THRYMIR!" they yelled. Each of the king's steps shook the very foundations of the castle.

There was one Yeti from a distant tribe of Jotun that never interrupted his meal, paying respect to the Jotun king. He was larger and more muscular than any of the other Yeti, but it didn't matter. Thrymir laid one hand on his head. Squeezing down, the Yeti grasped the king's wrist and struggled in an attempt to get free. As Thrymir clenched his hand, blood and brains oozed between his giant fingers. He grabbed the limp and lifeless corpse before it hit the ground and tossed it onto the table of Yowie.

"Looks like Yeti is on the menu tonight!"

No Jotun dared to speak out or act against the king after this. Even the Yeti tribe kept quiet and returned to the feast when instructed.

Thrymir was the giant troll king that ruled Jotunheim through fear and power. He was imposing and bold but also a ruthless leader. He kicked and shoved any of the Jotun in his way to his large throne by the fireside.

Loki watched silently from the window's ledge at the monstrous horrors unfolding before him. Suddenly, a beautiful witch appeared from the back of the hall. She had a hauntingly beautiful aura that mysteriously masked a true lethal form. It was Verdandi, and she could sense Loki's presence. She walked among the Jotun with grace until she reached a throne by Thrymir's side.

Appearing unaware of the falcon by the window, she leant over and whispered delicately in the troll king's ear. Suddenly, he rose from his chair. "It appears we have an uninvited guest in my hall. Get him!" Thrymir snarled while directing everyone's attention to the window.

Immediately every Jotun attempted to grasp the bird, but Loki found fun in their failure. Hopping from surface to surface, like a falcon, he quickly moved around the hall. He avoided hairy palms and grasping claws with ease, becoming overconfident with his success. Loki liked making fools of anyone, but his cockiness got the better of him.

He landed near Thrym's throne, and Verdandi shot a web from her hands at his feet. "Verdandi's magic has you stuck now, little Loki," Thrym snarled. Loki flapped hard, trying to free himself but was unable to move. Suddenly, his world became pitch black. Loki was entrapped in a box with no light and only a tiny amount of air to survive.

As time went on, his hope for freedom dwindled. Three long days and three long nights passed in slow succession. Loki's mind was tortured with despair as he starved. Thoughts of death while believing he had so much life kept him scarcely alive. Empty blackness and deafening silence allow his mind to wander into the darkest corners of the mind.

On the fourth day, Verdandi removed his prison cover and the light blinded the trickster. As his vision returned, his heart skipped a beat when he saw her. "Ah, my dear Loki. Look how far you've fallen since our last meeting," she seductively said, while Loki was weak from hunger and thirst.

"What do you want from me, my beauty?" He asked, barely being able to stand in his falcon form.

"Show me your true form Loki!" she demanded, releasing him from his cage.

Instantly, Loki shed the feathered falcon cloak and fell to the ground upon his release.

"There you are. I have a task for you, my dear Loki," She smirked.

"Name it," Loki replied in haste.

"Go back to Asgard and retrieve Thor. Deliver him weaponless to Thrymir's keep," she replied.

"How?" Loki asked. "He doesn't like the Jotun, and an attempt to attack him will result in death.".

Verdandi began to consider her plans. "A promise of the heart. The quickest way to a young warrior's heart is through their loins. Thrymir has two daughters. I will gift them magical abilities to make Thor's journey fatal. He will be ready to accept their warm embrace and receive the cold embrace of death herself," she said, pleased with her devious plot.

Thrym entered with his two daughters. "Behold, Tanngrisnir and Tanngnjóstr! My two beautiful daughters." With a wave of Verdandi's hands and a few magical incantations, the daughters became empowered with beauty and the ability to use magic.

Loki was supplied with enough food and drink to regain his strength for the flight home.

"If my daughters fail, Verdandi, I won't," Thrym vowed.

"I'll hold you to that, my mighty king. Thor's end will mark the end of Asgard," Verdandi sinisterly grinned as Loki disappeared into the distance.

Yule Goats

After Loki soared through the skies, he landed back in Asgard, weak, exhausted and drained. He was bound by oath to Verdandi to cause problems for the Aesir. Returning the falcon cloak to Freya, he had a sad look on his face. "What is wrong, my son?" she asked.

"I found her, mother. But she wants me to deceive Thor," Loki shrugged.

"Not near the sea, is it, son?" Freya probed.

"No, mother. It is in Suttung's old keep. It is now Thrymir's castle.".

"Go fetch Thor, Loki. It may be a lesson he needs.".

Rushing around the village of Asgard, Loki found Thor boasting of his triumphs in Ireland. "After I slew the giant, I bedded the one he built the causeway for. Jarnsaxa, I think her name was" Thor boasted among a few female nymphs and elves. "Ah, Loki! Two legs, I see, better than eight, eh, Sleipnir," Thor chuckled.

"Ah yes, funny. Anyway, you boast of glory and love conquests, and I thought to bring you news from Jotunheim. There are a couple of beautiful maidens that are eager to meet you. Thrymir's daughters," informed Loki.

"Thrymir! What does that troll want from me?".

"Nothing Thor, honestly. I've just come from his place, and he gave me the best meal I've had in days."

"Let us go then, Loki. Let me grab some weapons," Thor said as he stood up.

"No weapons required, good Thor. Thrymir has sworn that no trouble will come to us in Jotunheim," Loki said quickly to ease Thor.

"Let's be on our way then, Loki. Try not to offer your rear as a gift this time." Loki glared at Thor as he chuckled through his joke.

Over the Bifrost and into Midgard, the pair travelled on foot to the vast mountainous terrains. The journey was long and challenging, up steep rocks and through the clouds. Each steep step took them into denser fog-like mists. They began feeling the strenuous difficulties of travelling by foot. Scaling the mountains beyond the clouds, they finally made it to Thrymir's vast lands in Jotunheim.

Tired and exhausted from the climb, they took a moment to rest for an hour. After nourishing themselves on a delicious apple from Idunn's orchard, their journey continued. It wasn't long before they stumbled across a quaint little cottage in Jotunheim. It belonged to Gridr, a former lover and mother to Vidar. She guided and welcomed them with the offer of shelter and food.

There were many exchanges of laughs and stories over the table. Gridr even spoke of me in my younger days over the meal shared and mead drunk. Thor Boasted of victory and trials overcome against Jotun witches and ogre warriors. The night got late, and Loki retired from the feast exhausted with a full belly and tired legs.

"Thor Odinson, I have gifts for your journey. Take these three items. They will help you on your journey. And heed my warning, boy. Thrym is under the control of Verdandi. They both do not wish good things for Odin and his kin," Gridr warned, handing him the items.

The first item gifted was Jarngreipr, a pair of iron gauntlets that provided their wearer protection from burns and extra aid with extra grip. The second was Megingjord. A belt that gives the wearer double their strength. Combining the power of the belt with Thor's already impressive strength, he'd be able to lift the weight of the sky higher than any other.

"Now, this item I will need back, young Thor. It is my staff and it will keep your footing sure. No matter the surges you may experience or battles you may face. Keep steady and balanced and victory will be yours," Gridr handed over her staff and smiled. "Now get some rest, Thor. You will need your energy for the journey ahead."

The following day they woke early to continue their journey deeper into the heart of Jotunheim. The lands were tranquil and peaceful, with no Jotun crossing their path towards Thrymir's keep. They travelled through dark forests and rocky trails until Thor and Loki had to cross a shallow river with a deep embankment. It was ankle deep and didn't appear too threatening for them to navigate.

They climbed down the steep riverside and stepped into the cold crisp water. The mossy covered rocks and currents, in some parts, increased the threat of dangers. The gentle flow of a stream, if not approached with caution, will run rapidly over the top of you when the waters begin to rush.

Thor wielded the staff to steady himself while Loki carefully held onto his belt. Carefully, they began to cross slowly. They were midway when the waters began to recede. Confused, both shrugged their shoulders and travelled with a bit more ease.

Suddenly, all went quiet. A muffled sound in the distance replaced Jotunheim's tranquil sounds of nature. They both searched for the source, scanning their surroundings but neither could find anything. Finally, they looked up the river and identified the origin of the strange sound. A tsunami of water flowed, almost blotting out what little light the sun gave.

As the water rushed toward them like a stampede of wild water horses, Thor stood his ground. The onslaught of Bækhest galloping toward him was enough to terrify the bravest of heroes but Thor had courage. Plunging Gridr's staff into the ground, he braced himself. Loki attempted to scramble away, but Thor's gauntlets pulled the fool close while maintaining a firm grip on the staff. The water rushed but parted when it met Thor standing strong against the rapids.

All three gifts work in perfect synchronisation. The staff parted the water. Jarngreipr held Loki tightly, and Megingjord amplified Thor's might against the powerful surging waters. He lifted Loki high above the water level. Peering, he saw the most beautiful maiden standing on the side they were headed. Loki screamed, asking for help, but the maiden's gaze remained unaffected by his distress.

Pulling Loki back to his belt, Thor urged him to hold it tightly. Loki yelled above the sounds of the rushing water engulfing them, informing Thor of the maiden on the bank. Bending over, Thor picked up a small stone and hurled it toward her. It flew toward her at an incredible pace, striking her head. It knocked her to the ground, and soon after, the waters receded once more. As the pair scrambled to the side, they located the stone, but there was no beautiful maiden. Thor and Loki continued on their travels.

They approached Thrym's castle, and the large creaky doors opened very slowly. The stench of death was in the air. Thor was separated from Loki by a Jotun. The Yowie guided Thor to a secluded room. Down the long dark corridors with cobwebbed corners, it wasn't the warm welcome Thor expected. All that this room contained was a chair and two large goats and one of them had a cut on its head.

Thor patted the goats before taking a seat and resting his legs. The harmless goats came to each side of his chair, eager for attention. Thor remained calm by patting them. One bared its teeth like a strange smile at Thor, while the other ground its teeth, enjoying some dry straw lying on the floor.

Unexpectedly, the chair began to rise rapidly. The goats weren't what they appeared; they were Thrym's daughters—lifting the chair until the ceiling crushed Thor. Thor had to think quickly and with Gridr's staff gripped tightly, with his iron gauntlets, he braced himself. The daughters bleated while pushing with all they had, but Thor's strength proved their equal.

As the three struggled for victory, Megingjord began to glow. Thor felt the power flow from the belt into his muscles. His strength now doubled and proved to be too much for the daughters of Thrymir. Thor gave one mighty push against the ceiling until a crack echoed. The daughters of Thrym snapped under the pressure of Thor's resilience. Their spines broke, causing the pair to perish immediately.

Thor left the room with the corpses of the beautiful maidens on the floor. His temper began to blaze like his fiery red hair. He marched toward the feasting halls of the troll king. Thrym rose from his chair laughing. "You can't be Thor. You are too little and too puny. What is your name, little man?" Thrym asked.

"My name is eye, Thrym," Thor replied.

"Eye? That's a strange name, little man," Thrym chuckled as he picked Thor up. He walked toward the central fireplace as the rest of the Jotun feasted. The hall was full of monstrous warriors distracted by the feast in front of them.

Sharp toothed Yowies, giant footed sasquatch, trolls and ogres devouring something putrid. As Thor scanned the room, he realised human flesh was the source of the monsters' sustenance. Legs, arms and entrails provided the foul Jotuns meat and stirred something deep inside Thor.

Thor's anger raged inside, causing Jotunheim to darken with thunderous clouds. He maintained a calm expression as the thundercloud began to rumble. Thor carefully plotted his next move, spotting Loki by the exit. "I prefer my humans cooked," Thrym grunted as he began to put Thor closer to the flame.

This enabled Thor to execute his plan flawlessly. He stretched and grabbed an ember with his iron gauntlets and hurled it towards Thrym. With a bellowing roar, Thrym clutched his eyes in anguish. The hall echoed with the cries of pain as Thor fell to the ground. The Jotuns looked up from their meals to find out what happened to their king but he was in too much pain to speak.

Thor escaped unchallenged as all were distracted. Grabbing Loki, he returned to the room of the dead maidens. "Loki, get us out of here! And quick!" Thor advised as he scrambled to find a way out. beneath a pile of straw, where he found a giant cart. "Now, all we need is a couple of horses," Thor told Loki.

At that moment, Loki looked at the dead bodies of the beautiful maidens. He waved his hands and cast the resurrection spell that I had cautioned against. The beautiful girls reverted to their giant goat form. "Behold your noble steeds! Tanngrisnir and Tanngnjóstr!" Loki hailed. They were not the same as before, unable to change back to Jotun form but gained another unique ability. With enough electrical energy, if they fell, their lives would be restored.

Thor and Loki departed Jotunheim in haste, and when Thrymir was able to speak to the army, it didn't help. The sound of Thrymir's pain still echoed in the hall. Verdandi entered after hearing the king's anguish. "Is it done? Did you kill Thor?".

"No," he replied through the wailing.

"Who did this?" the witch questioned further. The sobbing slowly turned to a whimper.

"Eye did it! Eye was responsible!" he yelled to the room of puzzled Jotun.

Verdandi screamed like a banshee killing the Jotuns in the hall. Her scream could be heard for miles but was only fatal to those nearby. Loki looked back, heartbroken with Verdandi's pain. It seemed she would be forced to find other methods to bring Asgard to its knees.

The Elven Workshops

Love or difficulties in love can cause people to stew and be self-destructive. Love is the prize we all should hope to achieve in the end, good host. Moments are enhanced when love has been accomplished, but that can be related to both ways, the joys and the pain.

Loki had stewed on Thor for some time while plotting devious plans. "Thor kept me from my Verdandi. He will pay," Loki vowed while pacing up and down in his room. That was when he had conjured an answer to his revenge.

It was a peaceful night in Asgard as Mani pulled the moon across the sky. His horses left the dew on the ground as they galloped hard and fast, keeping Skoll at a safe distance. Drool from Hrimfaxi would cover the worlds below and even leave frost in the early hours of the day. Everyone was sound asleep, well, almost everyone.

The next day Sol illuminated the skies like the joy on someone's face brightens your day. Everyone stretched and yawned as they woke safely behind Asgard's walls. All appeared well until clarity came to the mighty thunderer's vision.

"Loki!" Thor called as the skies trembled. Each footstep shook the skies as Thor marched towards Loki's room. It took three powerful knocks on Loki's doors before Thor's rage soared higher. After a while, with no reply, he pushed through, shattering the doors to find the trickster waking from his slumber.

"Why? Why did you defile my beautiful Sif?" Thor asked, picking the tired Loki up from his bed.

As he dangled, struggling to breathe, he gargled, "what are you talking about?".

Thor threw him to the wall and asked again. "Why did you cut her hair?"

Loki's face knew what Thor spoke of despite trying to conceal his involvement. "You kept my love from me at Thrym's keep," Loki snarled back from the floor.

"We were going to die, Loki. Thrymir would have eaten us both, you fool."

"It wasss only you that she wanted dead," Loki growled back.

Thor walked toward Loki more forcefully. "Fix this! Odin may have the oath to protect your life, but that won't stop me from inflicting pain on it," Thor threatened.

"A hat or a scarf would fix it, Loki suggested sarcastically.

"Perhaps if I begin to break your bones, you'll come up with a more suitable answer," Thor suggested as his temper rumbled the beautiful blue skies in Asgard.

By the time Thor reached the third finger, Loki's pain had become unbearable. "I'll go to the elves! They can fix Sif's hair, and I'll get back into your good gracesss with another gift!" Loki rushed to say before Thor could grab another finger.

"Very well, Loki, but if I am not pleased, I will return to breaking your bones. I enjoy watching you suffer."

Loki ran as fast as he could to Eir. He would require his hand to mend to calculate his next move.

The second stop was the workshop that belonged to the sons of Ivaldi. They were elven craftsmen from my bloodline, and they loved to work with gold. Loki approached them first as their lineage had already assured their loyalty.

"Sons of Ivaldi, the gods are holding a grand competition to see who the better craftsmen are. Who can make the fairest of gifts? The sons of Ivaldi or the mysteriously dark Brokkr and Eitri? Oh yes, but one of your gifts will have to be long strands of golden hair that mimic the real thing," Loki informed the elves in the workshop.

"Sure, we can do that. We have three in mind: one for Odin, another for Freyr, and the last is for Thor's wife," the elves replied.

"How did you know about Sif?".

The brothers began to chuckle amongst themselves. "If Thor's voice rumbling the Skylands wasn't enough, your whimpering did the trick. Get out of here, Loki! We have work to do."

Loki departed Asgard to locate the dark inn amidst the gloomy forest. It was called Fjalar's Inn, and all beings of dark nature were welcomed there. Loki cautiously checked his surroundings as he approached the bar. The room was filled with grunts and snarls from Jotuns of all lands. The goblins grinned at Loki, and their gaze followed him slowly as he approached the bar.

"Aaahemm!" Loki tried to gain the bartender's attention. The room when quiet, and everyone's attention turned to Loki. "I'm looking for the craftsmen called Brokkr and Eitri. Have you seen them?" Loki asked the barkeep.

"Brokkr and Eitri... Yes, I've heard of them, but what do you want?" the barkeep asked.

"A competition for the gods. The greatest three gifts will earn them honour and glory in all the nine realms," Loki stated.

"Well, I'm Eitri, and I'm not interested in serving the gods," the barkeep replied.

"Eitri? I thought you were Fjalar, the owner of this establishment.".

"That was a name in another life, Loki. If we were to compete, we would require a price higher than honour and glory of the gods," Eitri smirked.

"Scared, are we? I would be too. The sons of Ivaldi are great craftsmen and are unbeatable. I'd bet my head on it," Loki foolishly claimed.

"Deal. We could use a head like yours, Loki. It would please Verdandi.".

Loki nervously gulped as he had made a wager he wasn't prepared to keep. The inn returned to its usual ruckus as Jotun, goblin and dwarf returned to drinking.

Loki cautiously scanned the room while at the bar. Human remains were torn and shared between the Jotun. Goblins spilled their ale while gambling with gold and the Dwarves remained disgusted by them all. They stayed quiet in the corner, far from any chance of action. However, if a Jotun or goblin ever approached with bad intention, they would become intimately acquainted with a sharp axe.

There appeared to be regular competition in the centre. A red cap dwarf guzzling blood and using his hat to clean the residue from his mouth. He was a little shorter than most humans, but he had a strong presence in the room.

He had a line of opponents from his table to the door, competing in an arm-wrestling competition. A Jotun, considered big and strong from all species, challenged him but none came close to victory. The red cap dwarf slammed fist after fist into the table. Groans of agony followed soon after.

"Hail me! Brokkr, the strongest in the nine realms!".

Loki heard the cheers of victory over his shoulder, sending a spine-chilling feeling throughout his entire body. Nervously leaving the establishment to return to Asgard, he began plotting and planning his escape from the oath made to Eitri.

Manufacturing the Gifts

Immediately after the terms were set, the sons of Ivaldi began their work. One of them threw a massive bar of gold into the forge. The blazing heat melted the gold brick into a red-hot liquid. The little elves, with their little tools, created the first gift. They worked with accuracy and speed, imbuing the item with magical properties.

It was fine golden strands that were so delicate they made the most beautiful blonde hairs look dull in comparison. Golden strands of beautiful blonde hair like a beautiful wheat crop during the harvest. It had roots to implant themselves into the desired person's head. The strands were so fine the gentlest of breezes made them float freely, almost like they would dance to the whistles of the wind. Loki looked on, pleased that Ivaldisons had corrected his mistake. This magical gift was both beautiful and bountiful. It was an incredible gift of wonder and awe.

The next item was made from a smaller piece of gold and just like before, It was thrown into the flames in the blazing forge. The gold burned hot and melted to a glowing red dripping liquid.

As the brothers carefully removed the liquid gold from the blaze, it dripped and burned a hole straight through the floor. The brothers were more careful carrying it to the anvil. The clinking and clanking overpowered magical incantations as they worked the metal. They used smaller tools to make quick work of this item. It was a magnificent golden armband with an intricate design of a dragon engraved. It was a grand gift that held both beauty and sentimentality.

The last item was the most remarkable out of the three. It was a great boar skin bigger than the size of a man. As soon as they pulled it from the forge with the liquid gold, the clinking and clattering filled the room. Each of the brothers worked with great effort as they fused each and every individual hair with the brightest and purest of the precious metal. The bristles became shiny and bright, illuminating the forge like a sunrise on a cold and frosty morning. It would be both wonderful and beneficial to the great king of Alfheim.

These three great golden gifts manipulated Loki into a false sense of comfort with their appeal and value. Gold will always be bright, shiny and of value but it will never be worth more than friendship and it tends to leave you quicker than it comes.

To ensure his head remained in its place, Loki would have to go deep into the heart of Svartalfheim. In between the border of Jotunheim and Midgard lies the dark elf tavern and Brokkr and Eitri's forge. Loki would have to rely on his cunning and clever tricks to ensure it remained attached to his neck.

Loki hid amongst the trees outside the dark elven forge. The day was grey and the night was black. The sound of trees bending and sticks snapping filled the air. Jotun grumbles and groans and sinister goblin giggles surround Loki as the wind whistles and the light from Fjalar's inn beaconed them closer.

As the sounds became louder, Loki became fearful of discovery. Thinking quickly, he shapeshifted and snuck into the forge. Brokkr and Eitri were enhanced with Verdandi's magic and blood from the mead of poetry. Their senses were heightened, and they could feel an unusual presence in the forge.

The faint buzzes of the fly caused them irritable headaches until the fly came to rest. Grabbing their ears, they tried swatting at Loki but were unsuccessful. Loki decided to give them relief for moments, only to assess their work from a safe distance on the wall.

These unique abominations of the dark elves observed many things in their pursuit of prey. They crept in the shadows, from the docks to the blacksmith's forge in kingdoms far and wide, discovering beautiful sources of inspiration. Due to their nature, they became inspired by items that drew blood. Steel blades sharper than their fangs. Hard iron that hit harder than the stone dropped on Gilling's Wife. Beautiful boats that could carry many over water to explore uncharted lands. Loki had a real cause for worry as it was not only the beauty of the craftsmanship but the incredible amount of application of such gifts that might determine the victor.

The first of the trinkets they would create was for Freyr. It was a magical cloth that could be unfolded and placed into the oceans. It was a ship that could be transported over land while he walked through Midgard to Alfheim and provided enough room for the council of gods to sail the seas. An excellent toy for a king of elves and fairies.

The second item the vampiric goblins made for the competition was my mighty spear. The shaft was manufactured from the wood of the mighty Yggdrasil. It was magnificent. Straight and smooth with my name carved into the pole linking it with me and I with it. It was beautifully crafted, providing both wonder and awe. It was versatile, providing a safe distance while defending. It could be offensive and extremely deadly to my enemies when thrown from afar. A multipurpose tool that also offers easy concealment as a walking staff or stick or, in modern times, a cane.

Eitri used a hammer and tongs to beat the steel to a fine point sending sparks flying through the forge. Brokkr bore the burden of the bellows, pumping in perfect timing to ensure the temperature remained constant. Not a fraction hotter or cooler than needed; otherwise, the gifts would be imperfect. Each pump required the unnatural and unmeasurable strength of Brokkr.

Quietly admiring the brothers' work, Loki had an idea to ensure his victory. He only had one chance to execute his devious plot and no matter what, he had to ensure perfection wasn't the outcome.

Eitri heaved a large clump of iron to the forge burning hotter than Muspelheim. Flames blazed as they danced among the hot coals. From the outside, the dark forest lit up from its usual gloomy and creepy existence. Trolls, ogres, and goblins shielded their eyes. This third item would be a symbol of strength throughout the nine realms. A sign that would make trolls and monsters think twice before ever crossing someone who wore it.

"Now remember, Brokkr, not a fraction of a degree hotter or cooler.".

"Yes, yes! Otherwise, our victory won't be guaranteed! I know!"

Brokkr began pumping, evenly paced and not a degree higher or lower than required. Eitri left while Brokkr continued to pump the fiery forge. He used his sense of touch to measure the temperature by the sweat on his brow. Heaving and pushing the heavy bellows provided the wind to make embers explode into a wildfire. Each groan Brokkr made showed the amount of strain the great bellows in dark forge required.

Loki decided it was time to make his move. He buzzed around the room, circling Brokkr in the forge. Brokkr strained his face as he suffered the sound. It was like nails on a chalkboard with heightened senses but Loki ended his discomfort. He landed on Brokkr's hand and bit down hard. Brokkr yelled out in anguish and pain, but it did not hinder his pace.

Loki circled the room again, knowing Brokkr could not stop to swat him away. He landed on Brokkr's neck, biting even harder than before. It caused the blood to flow from his wound like a river running rapidly to his shoulder. His agony could be heard throughout Svartalfheim. However, he did not stop or slow his pace.

Loki became infuriated with his failure to hinder Brokkr and Eitri's attempt to claim his head. Seeing the ticks in Brokkr, he buzzed closer to the dark elf's ears. Brokkr twisted his neck and ground his teeth in frustration at the fly. Loki did this for a while, causing Brokkr to lose concentration. Landing on the eyelid, Brokkr twitched and jerked, trying to get the fly off. Loki was unfazed, almost relishing annoying Brokkr.

"Keep the pace steady!" Eitri called from the other side of the room.

Loki steadied his footing on Brokkr's eyelid. Opening his mouth as wide as a fly could, Loki bit down for the third time. Bone-chilling screams that would curdle the blood of mortals sent the ravens flying from the forest's floor. Brokkr yelled out in pain as the blood blinded him.

"Keep the forge steady!" Eitri called out above the screams. The blood and pain in Brokkr's eye forced him to stop pumping. The annoying buzz kept him from focusing on his task. The forge stopped long enough to reduce the temperature by a fraction of a degree. The clinking of the iron that filled the forge was replaced with a large twang. Something had broken due to the temperature change.

After finishing his work, Eitri was displeased with his brother's efforts. "Oh well, I guess we'll have to see who wins the contest now, brother," Eitri said, displeased with his tainted flawless work. It now was up to the magical abilities imbued in the unique toys for the gods to dictate the competition's winner. Loki left the forge confident in his sabotage.

Blitzen

Three days had passed since the challenge was set. The beautiful, bright brothers from Alfheim appeared first in Valhöll to present their wares. Three golden trinkets were carefully made and imbued with magic specific to each of the gods judging the competition. The items were covered but you could see a bright glow from underneath.

Loki stood in the hall pleased with his efforts to hinder Eitri and Brokkr from winning. Thor, Freyr and I lined up in anticipation of the reveal of the great items, but the goblin brothers appeared to be missing. "What gifts do you bring, good elves? You might as well present them to us while we wait for the others," I smiled, impressed by their efforts.

"Yes, I get to keep my head," Loki mumbled.

"You bet your head Loki? You fool! This contest is yet to be judged, and the goblins still have time," I scorned, causing Loki's grin to fall from his face.

The elves stepped forward, each carrying one of the three gifts. The Ivaldisons presented the first gift, and it was the golden hair intended for Sif. "This gift, once attached, will grow just like hair. Its roots will go deep, and its beauty will enchant the crops to grow. Its last ability is to restore the loveliness of your wife, Thor. She will be just as beautiful as before," one of the sons of Ivaldi claimed.

Thor looked pleased. He placed it on his wife's head and each root took hold. The golden hair gleamed, bringing joy to both Thor and Sif, and relief to Loki.

The next gift presented was for me. It was a golden arm band called Draupnir. "It is wonderful, but what does it do?" I asked, curious about its magical properties.

"Well, Odin, this arm ring increases the wealth and value of its wearer. It shares the same abilities as wisdom and knowledge. Every ninth night it drips eight identical arm rings, which can be used as tokens to share or wealth to store good King," the elf proudly said.

"It is good, but wealth and knowledge does not contribute to ones worth in life. It is more valuable to share what you can for developing kinship. Thank you for the gift, good elf," I said to Loki's upset. He began to look nervous, worried about his wager.

The last gift was for Freyr, and it was a golden boar skin called Gullinbursti. Freyr's eyes lit up at such a fantastic gift. "What does it do?" The young king asked in excitement.

"Well, good King and Lord of all the Elves, this skin provides its wearer extraordinary magical abilities. It will provide you with the ability to travel over land and sea when it is in boar form. The skin's golden hair will light up the darkest nights providing hope in times of despair. You will become the great boar warrior of all the realms, striking fear in the hearts of those that challenge you. Lord Cernunnos, you will be our guiding light in the darkness," the elf said as he handed over the gift.

"I love it!" Freyr shouted, giddy like a child during Yule.

Loki's worry dissipated as two of the three gifts left him confident of his victory in the wager. Unknown to him, emerging from the shadows, the two goblin brothers appeared with their items. The sound of metal scraping the ground filled my hall. Brokkr's eye was swollen from Loki's bite, and Eitri did what he could to help him.

"You are too late, Brokkr and Eitri," Loki smirked.

"Now, now Loki, do not be too hasty to claim the victory when it is I that is in charge of this hall."

Brokkr placed the first gift gently in front of Freyr. He snorted, wiping his nose as he took a few steps back. "What is it? A piece of cloth?" Freyr asked disapprovingly.

"Lord Cernunnos, this is Skidbladnir. An offering of extraordinary ability. It folds small like a piece of cloth that can fit inside your pocket. However, once it is unfolded, it becomes the greatest of all ships. No matter the season, it will always have the wind on its side," Brokkr grunted.

"Oh, this is great!" Freyr told the brothers, giving Loki reason to worry once more.

Eitri stepped forward, placing the next gift in front of me. "This is Gungnir, the greatest of all spears. Anyone who swears an oath with it then the oath will be magically upheld. It is straight to the point with its shaft carved out of the wood from the mighty Yggdrasil. Once thrown, it will never miss its target no matter how far it may be.".

"A great gift indeed goblin of Verdandi," I said, causing Loki's panic to grow. "Bring on the final gift," I told Brokkr and Eitri.

Both brothers heaved the final gift until it was in front of Thor. "A hammer, but its handle is too short. It appears I have received the worst gift of all," the mighty thunder god claimed.

"How wrong you are, Thor. This hammer is Mjolnir, and it is the greatest weapon in the nine realms. It is unbreakable, and when thrown, it will always find its way back to your hand, thanks to the Vegvesir scribed on its head. It can also alter its size to fit the purpose of the wielder. It can shrink to hide your identity amongst humans, and it can grow to a size that could send Ymir flying with one blow. It is the lightning to accompany you, thunder god, and it will serve you well," Brokkr informed, straining through his injuries.

"Well, by Odin's eye, that is the greatest gift of all. The handle is nothing more than a minor detail in comparison to its abilities. Well done, little goblins. Well done," Thor's voice boomed with pride.

Thor, Freyr and I huddled together to discuss who had won the contest. Loki's panic grew into pacing up and down the hall. The elves thought they had one, while the goblins also stood confident. Loki's sweat beaded down the very thing he wagered, but after much discussion, the outcome was decided.

"Freyr, Thor and I have decided the victors. The elves of Alfheim, while your wares were valuable gold and riches, are superficial and do not determine the greatness of a god or a human. Fortunes come and go in time but are more likely to attract enemies than gain allies. Brokkr and Eitri, your gifts were very impressive indeed. Weapons provide the wielder protection, and a boat is beneficial to many gods that wish to travel over the oceans. A gift for one that benefits the many. You are the victors of the challenge today," I smiled and gave them all a nod of approval, impressed by their efforts.

Loki became clammy, and the colour of his face became a ghostly white. "Now for my payment Loki. And my revenge for you nitpicking at me while trying to produce the gifts," Brokkr moved closer with a sharp axe in hand.

"Wait, wait, wait! I did offer my head for a wager, but I did not mention damaging my neck," Loki slyly grinned. "You can only have my head if you do not damage my neck.".

Brokkr became displeased with Loki's words, and his axe dropped. He began walking towards me to discuss an alternate prize. He whispered in my ear the terms he wished to replace the agreed terms with Loki. All seemed fair, and it would serve as a lesson to Loki. Brokkr pulled out a magical iron wire from his pocket as he walked towards Loki. Loki backed away slowly, but suddenly, Eitri was behind him. One brother held the fool while the other began his horrible work.

"Loki let this be a lesson for you. Never wager that which you can't afford to lose. Best to keep your mouth shut to avoid situations like this," I said while he squirmed. Brokkr finished sewing his mouth shut so that his fork tongue could not deceive another.

Everyone left my hall that day happy with the gifts we had received, but Loki had to endure silence for three days before I removed the wire from his mouth. This magical wire I could repurpose at a later date. As no one can remove this wire, no one but me.

One Horse Open Sleigh

For a time, there was peace in Asgard, and all was well. Verdandi had to find a new way to bring my kingdom to its knees. She had trained Skadi for years in magics and warrior ability but was more calculated. Verdandi wished to crumble my empire from within before annihilating it. A king defeated by an enemy can rise again, but a kingdom that destroys itself can exercise again.

While I sat on Hlidskjalf, my gaze was drawn to a young Jotun within a mountainous landscape. He was unique and it was his appearance that provoked my curiosity. He was large like any mountain giant but made of flesh and stone. It was stone harder than regular boulders and if any other mountain giant challenged him, he would defeat them with ease.

I walked to the watery lake near Valhöll to find my horse. Its nature was overgrown and unkept. Moss grew on the trunks of trees and on top of the cold grey boulders scattered throughout. The trees had very little life in them as the branches wove amongst each other. I dipped my feet inside the icy cold, dark and murky water. Suddenly, a thick fog rolled over the water as the faint sounds of ripples filled the deathly silence. I could feel waves against my knees as the monstrous beast from the depths revealed itself.

The shapeshifting horse of death had decayed skin and teeth sharp enough to tear the flesh of any victim foolish enough to attempt to ride it near the water. It was a giant horse that only I could control, being a god of death. Four of the eight legs reared up from the murky water as my horse approached. Haunting neighs could be heard all over the sky lands in Asgard.

I strapped my eight-legged Kelpie called Prancer to the slippery one and left Asgard in haste. Eight legs galloped across the sky, water and land in quick succession towards the mountains. This cursed horse seemed to move faster than any other I had seen. It was beautiful and appeared normal to anyone who spotted it at first. However, when left unattended, it tricked victims onto the Kelpie's back; they would become stuck. It treated them the same as Loki treated it before. The beautiful horse revealed its terrible side and dragged the prey to the watery depths where they would feed on the soggy flesh.

Finally reaching our destination, the rock mountain giant was grooming his horse. "Hrungnir, I have been keeping my eye on you, boy. I'm curious about your origins as no Jotun before you has ever been birthed by Seidr from both flesh and stone," I asked while scanning his form in awe. He was a giant in the flesh but what he lacked in body parts, he made up for in an enchanted stone. A rock arm and legs made from stone, but it was his heart that genuinely grasped my attention. It was encased in stone, and it pounded harder than any drum.

"Odin, someone told me you would come by sooner or later. What might I tell you so you will leave me alone?".

"How did you become as impressive as you are?" I probed using flattery.

"I'll tell you what, Odin. If you and your monstrous horse can defeat me and my noble steed, I will tell you how I became the way I am."

I looked upon his steed and it looked magnificent. The magnificent mare had a coat with slight yellow colour and a beautiful golden mane. It was called Gulfaxi and I wanted the pretty mare to join my sleigh. "Ok, I agree, Hrungnir. A race for your story, and when we make it to Asgard, we will celebrate in feast and merriment among the other gods."

The terms were set, and we took our starting points. In a flash, Hrungnir started the race and took a quick lead. I flicked my reins which sent my Kelpie galloping away with my Sleipnir sliding behind. The winds rushed as we both raced towards victory.

It didn't take long before we caught up to Hrungnir and Gulfaxi. We had the advantage of quickly crossing water, while Gulfaxi slowed at every river we crossed. We trekked through the thick snowy mountains of Jotunheim and over the fields we went. We roamed at an incredible pace which proved my sleigh to be the better. It glided across the surface of the snow where Gulfaxi was a little more heavy-footed. We approached the end of Midgard and I called to Heimdall to call forth the Bifrost.

The beautiful rainbow appeared before us and we left the snow and land behind. Our horses galloped hard on the last leg of the race, but when we arrived at Valhöll, I was the victor. "Well done, boy. Let's share a meal and a tale inside once we have both freshened up," I panted.

I led my horse back to its dark and murky home, releasing it to return to its deadly depths. Gulfaxi was given hay and water for its efforts in the race by the Valkyrie. It wasn't long before Hrungnir and I were clean. The dirt from our fingernails and a fresh set of the finest clothes to be presented appropriately at the meal. I had even gifted Hrungnir some new garments so that he would feel welcomed at the feast.

After a few too many drinks, Hrungnir became more talkative and slurred his words. His story revealed that as a child, Verdandi gave him three hearts and enchanted the rocks around him to become limbs. Every three years, she would gift him more stone and clay to grow his appendages at the same rate as the flesh.

It was unfortunate he wasn't wise enough to know his limits with mead. The more he drank, the more he spoke of owing his life to Verdandi and her cause. Her plan revealed itself the more intoxicated Hrungnir got when he began boasting about Asgard's fall. Verdandi's web of wyrd became alarming because of how long a game she was prepared to play. I began to play back finally.

I sent Huginn, my trusty companion, to fetch Thor from his hall.

"I will pull Asgard from the skies and send it plunging into the ocean. Not before I take your Freya and Sif back to Jotunheim so they can know what it feels to be with a true champion of Jotunheim.".

I noticed Sif was at the table already and she became very uncomfortable. I asked him to politely stop before his poor attitude got him in trouble but trying to reason with a drunk fool will always be a fruitless chore. He refused my warning and if I were a lesser god, I would have run him through with Gungnir. Just as my grip tightened on my spear, Thor burst through the doors. Thunder roaring and lightning flashed in the background as his gaze met Hrungnir's as he was inappropriately grasping at his wife.

Thor marched straight up to Hrungnir, grabbing him by the throat, demanding he would stop. Hrungnir grinned arrogantly at Thor like a drunk fool. "I challenge you, Thor. If you are brave enough to face me in Jotunheim in three days," Hrungnir slurred.

Thor was taken back. No giant had ever been brave enough to challenge him in combat before. Impressed by Hrungnir's courage, Thor accepted the terms set by Hrungnir as he stumbled and staggered returning to Jotunheim. Hrungnir demanded three days to prepare so the victory would be his. Thor agreed because he had a reputation to maintain. He was the mighty hero of Asgard and almost unstoppable with his iron gauntlets, the belt of strength and the best of all hammers.

Three days had passed, and Hrungnir was ready. He created a colossal clay golem that stood higher than any mountain. It dwarfed the rest of the mountain giants and Hrungnir used one of his three hearts to give it life. It was enormous but it was in its infancy. It would have terrified most heroes, but Thor was not most heroes.

Over the mountains, in the distance, the clouds went from white to grey to black. Thor was furious at Hrungnir's disrespect when he was a guest in my hall. The mighty goats pulled Thor's chariot over the land and the dark clouds followed closely behind. The giant golem began to tremble with each step Thor took toward it. The golem quivered in fear and what was once stiff clay legs were replaced by a soggy base. The golem couldn't move because it ended up wetting itself.

"Shame it looked the part, but I guess it never had the right heart to fight," Thor boasted, causing Hrungnir to charge. He had a giant whetstone as his weapon, and the ground trembled as he rushed toward Thor. Hrungnir was no ogre or troll, Hrungnir was a mighty mountain giant, and Verdandi enchanted him with great power and strength. Thor remained unfazed as he drew Mjolnir from his belt. Hrungnir raised his whetstone about to bring it fatally down on Thor's head.

With a flash of lightning, Mjolnir left Thor's hand. It grew to a great size as it flew toward its target. It smashed the whetstone, sending shards flying in all directions but Mjolnir continued toward its target. It crashed through the rock only to be stopped by the crunching of Hrungnir's skull.

In the blink of an eye, the hammer returned to Thor's hand and moments after, a shard from the whetstone had struck Thor's forehead. While dazed, he did not see the headless body of Hrungnir stumble and fall toward him. Thor became trapped under the great weight of the leg, unable to free himself. Despite all this strength, he still required aid.

After struggling for some time, the gods attempted to free him. God after goddess and elf after dark elf, but none could free the mighty protector of Asgard and Midgard. It wasn't until I fetched his son with a Jotun maiden in Ireland.

Magni stepped forward at only three years old and he lifted the leg with all of his might. His father was finally free, and he gifted the youngster the great horse, Gulfaxi, as his reward. It was a fair reward for Thor's mighty Jotun boy.

Eir attempted to heal Thor, but the whetstone had a curse attached. The curse of arrogance. Thor became boastful of his great triumphs. After a while of claiming greatness, Eir left the stone in its place, and I would require more extraordinary magic to humble the mighty Thor.

The Grinch

A few years had passed since Hrungnir's demise. It was a still winter's night and there was peace was throughout all the regions. The snow drifted through the air and landed in the realms below. It was pure and untouched as all slept in the nine realms.

The humans gifted their children new clothes to keep the dangers of the cold away while preparing a celebration of their year's harvest. However, if I have learned anything in my years of life is that peace and tranquility never last long. It usually provides a distraction for your enemies to strike.

The following day proved me correct. Thor woke from his slumber troubled, as he had an unusual feeling. It was the feeling that something or someone unwelcome was in his bedchamber as he slept. As soon as Thor awoke, he reached over toward where his hammer was placed the night before. The air flowed through his fingers as he realised that it was gone. "LOKI!" he called out, shaking the entire realm. Loki woke and rushed to Bilskirnir, Thor's hall in Asgard.

"What isss it, Thor? I do not wish any bonesss to be broken today, ssso I came at once."

"Loki, you slippery little serpent! Are you a wolf in sheep's clothing? Are you completely clueless or trying to pull the wool over my eyes? I guess the only way to prove your innocence is to make you find what is lost."

After scanning the room, Loki quickly realised Mjolnir was taken. He was quick to offer his services to prove his innocence and save himself from pain. He left immediately to request Freya's help.

"Good day, mother. I require your falcon cloak. Thor'sss hammer is missing, and I have offered to find it for him."

"Last time, you almost got Thor killed by Thrym. Do you give me your oath this won't happen again," Freya spoke softly but was concerned about her son's intentions.

"Yesss, mother, I only wish to locate Thor'sss hammer and if I can help return it, then that would be even better."

Freya handed Loki the falcon cloak, despite her concerns. He left Asgard swiftly, flapping his wings, launching him into the air. He soared through the clouds over Midgard, frantically flying, trying to find Thor's weapon. Village to village and through the forests, he asked all the beings that crossed his path. The fairies never knew, the humans were also clueless, but the elves of Alfheim spoke of whispers and rumours from Jotunheim.

Whispers of a spider witch sneaking beyond the walls of Asgard, existing in the shadows of the darkest nights that had great speed and even greater stealth. It was Verdandi that snuck into Thor's room. It was her that took the hammer for another. She caused the hero discomfort in his restless night. She sat on his chest, tormenting his mind with terrors and froze his body stiff with sleep paralysis. That is how the hammer was taken. It was the weakening of Thor that lessened his ability to defend Asgard.

As soon as Loki heard her name, he flew directly to Jotunheim to locate her. Rapidly through clouds and swooping down through forests. He soared swiftly to the mountain's edge at Thrymir's kingdom. The winds whistled while his heart raced hunting the Jotun witch.

The green grass at the forest's edge changed to slimy wet mud. Before accessing Jotunheim, Loki questioned the dark elves further in an attempt to gather ideas to manufacture a plan. The dwarves informed Loki that Verdandi stole the hammer for another. A great Jotun King with poor sight. He alone knows of the hammer's location. Loki left the dwarven caves to continue his journey to Jotunheim.

Loki left the mud and clay behind and began his ascension into Jotunheim. The ground became barren of life the higher he flew. Vegetation on the trees became sparse until there were no trees left.

Nothing but rock and stone with air so thin it would make the mortals from Midgard disoriented and docile.

Up the mountain, he went until there stood a familiar sight. The vast castle that Loki had encountered before, Thrym's keep, stood tall and imposing amongst his kingdom but appeared quieter than before. The last time he visited, the sounds of grunts and roars filled the air, but now there was silence.

He flew over the wall and returned to his original form immediately. A familiar voice came from a familiar face in front of him. "Ah, Thor, are we missing something? A hammer, perhaps? It has been a long time and my sight is not what it used to be. I have you to thank for this. You look thinner than you used to. I'm shocked your puny form can even wield such a weapon," Thrym grunted.

Loki was taken back by the troll's poor vision. He would have to be blinder than a bat to think Loki's small frame could be Thor's. Changing his voice to Thor's to keep up with the illusion, Loki probed the Troll king for the hammer's location. "Why did you take it? Did you not learn last time our paths crossed. Did you think I'd allow you to claim my weapon," Loki said furiously, imitating Thor.

"If you want it back, I am willing to trade. I had a love of a powerful witch before, and I think I'd like that again with another. Odin's Freya for the hammer, those are my terms. Otherwise, you can return to Asgard and I'll keep the hammer forever out of your reach."

Loki left that horrible place and flew directly back to Asgard. After returning Freya's cloak, he approached me to convene a council meeting of the gods. I wanted to help indirectly, as a leader should. I blew my horn, alerting the others that a gathering at Valhöll was required. All the gods came immediately as Asgard's protection was vital to me.

Each god rushed from their halls to gather in Asgard in my hall. Each sat in their respective chair as the Einherjar were training. It was Thor's thunderous voice that filled the silence at my table.

"That grinch, Thrym, stole my hammer!"

"Asgard needs its champion and his weapon," I told the room.

"What does he want?" Freyr asked.

"He wantsss to trade Freya for the hammer'sss return," Loki hissed.

The ground in my hall began to tremble as Freya's cats sought shelter. I could see rock slides and avalanches from my high throne as Freya seemed displeased. "We will not give Freya to this monster. She is far too valuable to me and I refuse even to consider using her to bargain," my voice boomed, silencing the others.

"What else can you tell us, Loki?" Njord asked.

"He was so blind that he thought I was Thor. Naturally, I changed my voice to match, but I found it quite odd."

"There you have it, Thor will go to Thrymir dressed as Freya," Heimdall suggested.

"I will not! I am a great warrior with many victories over the Jotun. Why can't I go to Thrym and slay all who oppose me?" Thor boasted arrogantly from the cursed stone in his head.

"Thrym is a cruel but cunning Jotun, Thor. If he has hidden the hammer, then there is no guarantee that after his death, you will get it back," Tyr counselled.

"It has been decided then, boy. Go to Thrym as Freya and when you have received the hammer as a dowry, only then can you unleash your wrath," I said, looking directly at Thor's disappointed eyes.

"I will help in any way I can," Loki said to Thor.

The council dispersed and Thor and Loki made plans and preparations for reclaiming Asgard's mightiest weapon. Loki enjoyed diminishing Thor's powerful character with a dress, a veil and make-up. It appeared the vision I had at Fenrir's imprisonment was coming to be.

Thor's Wedding

Nine days had passed before Loki and Thor had set their plan into action. Thor, dressed in white, departed Asgard under a veil and a different name. Loki accompanied him disguised as a pretty handmaiden. They travelled across the skies pulled by Tanngrisnir and Tanngnjóstr in Thor's sturdy chariot. Each of the giant goats trotted hard across the heavens. They created intimidating rumbles amongst the clouds on their way to Jotunheim.

Thor looked incredibly foolish, dressed as a bride with only a veil covering his face. His bulky size mixed with the muscular tone of a mighty warrior was hard to conceal. His disguise would not be able to fool a child, but it didn't have to. It only had to deceive a blind troll king.

A delicate and dainty white dress with floral patterns in lace restricted the thunder god's movements. It forced him to move like a woman with the fear of revealing his true form before his hammer was reclaimed. The seams held on the verge of bursting. If he had not moved elegantly, he'd be standing naked for all to see, and the hammer would be forever out of reach.

Loki, on the other hand, was a master of deception. He could change his shape, size and sound at his own desire. He enjoyed the illusion of it all. Appearing as something he is not, to wither hearts and warp the minds of others. With the spell I gave to become Ratatoskr, he moulded it into his own variations. Nightmares and dreams, mixed with his twisted mind, usually ended with someone suffering as his means of entertainment. Unless you possessed an all-seeing eye, you would be left vulnerable to his deceptions.

The chariot travelled up the mountain until they finally reached the great castle. Loki warned Thor to allow him to do all the talking. Thor lacked the same level of deception as Loki and if Thrymir heard his voice, the quest would fail. After all, he was responsible for Thrymir's poor sight.

On their arrival, a giant bigfoot greeted them at the door. "You cannot be Freya. Your ankles are thick and your shoulders are broader than a mighty oak tree. Perhaps my brother likes that sort of thing. You have a few nice rings, my pretty. After this marriage is consummated, I'll take them as payment of protection."

Thor began to puff his chest only to be eased by Loki in disguise. "You are tired, Freya. Allow me to guide you to Thrymir's table with this soon-to-be sister-in-law's help. We ladies must look out for each other." The sasquatch guided them to the feasting hall while the pair pretended to be clueless about their surroundings.

As the giant wooden doors opened, Thor smiled, recalling his victory there. Loki nudged him back to their present situation. "Remember, my lady, let me do the talking," Loki said, adjusting the veil before taking their seats.

"Welcome, my beautiful bride-to-be. Forgive me, but my sight isn't what it used to be. Being in your presence makes my heart flutter all the same. Judging by the silence in my hall, the whispers and mumbles are the Jotun jealous of my wife-to-be," Thrym boasted.

None of the Jotun would be so bold as to share their concerns with the appearance of Thor as Freya. They were afraid of death by either Thor's or Thrymir's hand. In the end, their silence would guarantee their demise, as they all were fated to fall by Mjolnir.

"Bring the feast!" Thrymir's hideous sister roared.

As the banquet was set in front of guests and host, Thor's eyes widened with joy. He loved to feast so much that he had forgotten the purpose of his quest. He was salivating as his stomach grumbled in anticipation. Every kind of animal meat was prepared and placed with much care by the servants. There were delicacies and dishes from all corners of the land to win Freya's heart through her stomach.

Forgetting himself, Thor grumbled and drooled at the feast. Thrymir became weary at the manly groans, but Loki quickly eased him with a lie. Thor's uncomfortable dress expanded as he relaxed, and It was lucky Loki remained focused. He whispered into Thor's ear, making him aware of the severity of his mission. Recovering the greatest weapon in life requires strength, control, and guile.

Moments had passed before Thrymir declared the start of the celebration. Thor began to devour food at an alarming rate. He shovelled handfuls of fruit and vegetables underneath his veil. The thunderer scoffed meat from the bone and inhaled salmon and exhaled fish skeletons. His consumption started to cause Thrymir to turn suspicious as he heard the whispers amongst the guzzling of mead.

"Such a voracious appetite, future wife. I have never heard of anyone, let alone a female with such an insatiable hunger," Thrym declared, impressed.

"Yes, good king. My queen has starved herself for nine nights in anticipation of her wedding," Loki reassured softly.

"Ah, this pleases me. How about a kiss from my future queen?" Thrymir said before he leant over the table and lifted Thor's veil. He became startled as his vision made out two bloodshot eyes.

"Emm maiden, why are my bride's eyes so bloodshot and angry looking?"

"The goddess' anticipation for this day has robbed her from her sleep, good king. Perhaps we should consummate the union and give her rest at last," Loki grinned as Thor glared at him.

"Fetch the hammer and we shall make the union complete," Thrymir demanded.

His sister left the hall and returned moments later. Thor's eyes followed the hammer as it was walked around the room. The Jotuns became apprehensive, hoping their silence would spare them from their ill fate. The hairy big-footed sister placed the weapon on Thor's lap as the dark clouds rolled overhead. The rumbling of the skies enhanced the panic in the wedding guests.

"Let Asgard have their hammer, my love. We shall go to the bed chambers.".

Thor gripped tightly on his hammer's short handle as lightning cracked outside. "NO! It is time to die, you troll." Thor launched Mjolnir straight at Thrymir's head, and just like that, his life was over. With a flash of light, the hammer returned to his hand.

The Jotuns felt fear like never before and began to scatter. Thor eradicated them without mercy. He was acting out of character because of his damaged ego. The cursed stone in his head enhanced Thor's arrogance, and as a result, his actions were fueled with hatred and rage.

Once all the Jotuns lay dead in the hall, he grabbed the tongue of Thrym. He tore it from the troll's head and placed it in Midgard. It was a reminder to any Jotun that dared to speak of the time that Thor married a troll. Trolltunga was its name and it was placed in the beautiful lands of Norway.

They left that place and all in the nine realms knew to never speak of the time when Thor wore white. I even began to doubt Thor's nobility and honour. If I couldn't remove that stone by magic, I would have to humble him in other ways.

Seasons' Greetings

Everything has its seasons and love follows the same cycle. Whether it is the joy of a warm summer's day or the bitterness of the frosty winter morning, love is the same. The hope that a warm spring brings as life flourishes once more or the tired leaves falling from their glorious highs before the cold sets in.

Appreciate that each season is there to understand the contrast. Whether you are an ash or elm tree, everyone has their seasons. Be prepared to weather them all in the journey of creating a life together. If you wish to seek adventure, prepare to get lost. If you aspire to be a warrior, be prepared to endure wounds. If you want to be a lover, be ready for both.

Allow me to tell you of my engagement. It was in the springtime. The birds were singing as the cold chill of the winter air finally warmed. We chased each other among the lavender fields and the green grassy hillside meadows. Our children would defend our kingdom from any threat Verdandi could muster. I wanted to be unrestricted without the burden of plotting and control. I was free to be present with my Freya.

We frolicked amongst the mountains and the beautiful glens she created. She was known as the Cailleach in the place that would be now called Scotland. My favourite place to visit was Skye because of its solitude and magic. It has fairy pools and mounds barely touched by humanity. There were only sheep and hairy cows that looked majestic in the crisp blue skies and fresh breeze. Those cows sparked fond memories of the noble Audumla that fell so long ago to create this beautiful landscape. I would eventually gift it to the mortals when I taught them how to sail and build bridges, but before that, I'd enjoy it with the one I love.

"I wish this could last forever," Freya said, looking lovingly in my eyes.

"I do enjoy our moments together. You give me peace in a lifetime of war. You are my future, my lady."

"If only we could find a way to make peace with my witch of a sister, Verdandi, we could share more moments like this one."

"I fear she won't be happy until I am dead. Let's forget her at this moment. I only want to be here in mind and body, with you. I want to be blind to all threats and live in this perfect moment with you, my lady."

The moments you share with a loved one are far more precious than any amount of gold. You are rich in life when another enhances the journey, and you are honourable when their needs prioritise and guide your own.

"My lady, I have something for you, something of great beauty but it is nothing compared to yours. I must leave to get it, but if you find me when I'm lost, you'll have earned this gift. With it, I hope you'll accept my hand. You will not only be my lady but my beloved," I said, holding her lovely soft hands.

"Nothing would please me more, Odin. Wherever you go, I will follow. I will love you from now until Ragnarok comes."

"Follow me east as Ēostre until you meet the dwarf called Austri. Follow me north as Frau Holle until you meet Norðri. Head south as Bastet and find Suðri. Finally, head west as Coatlicue and find the dwarf Vestri. Once you have all the pieces, I will have your engagement gift, my lady."

We retired together that night and, in the morning, I was gone. She woke up panicked but also recalled my instructions. She prepared for her journey, packing lightly.

Freya headed east first, over land and ocean, bringing the springtime with her. Over hills and seas, she travelled in search of me. Spring turned to summer and autumn quickly followed. Time passed swiftly and the joy of the chase made my lady weary. I was happy her love drove her but if too much time passed, playing hard to get can wear down the purest of loves and turn a heart cold.

Wintertime had blanketed the land with the purest snow when she finally stopped. Her quest had become an afterthought when she came across a small bird. It was tiny and it was dead. The bird had frozen in the winter with no hope for life returning to it. My Freya became colder and as a result, life in the world would die as love got icier.

As a last-ditch effort to rekindle her purpose and joy, I became a legendary hare. I hopped and bounded over the snow until I met her frosty tears, dripping like snowflakes delicately landing on the dead bird. I gently brushed her ankle to comfort her and warm her spirit. The bird's death took my lady, so I would have to bring a gift—a gift to give her hope and rekindle her loving heart.

Beneath my belly and on top of my feet, I was carrying an item. It was insignificant to most, but it would be the reason spring came around each year. It was a small delicate egg—the bird's egg that died. The present was a simple token that reminded Freya of the nature of things. The egg reminded her that life had to continue so that death would not be the end. Her cold heart thawed and began to flutter again.

As the spring returned to the land, so did the wildlife. As the snow receded, flowers began to blossom. Joyful hope returned to the realms and Freya. I couldn't help but smile as her beauty returned to light the world up once more. The animals and insects danced around her.

She looked up, through the swarm of wildlife, to discover the door of Austri appeared. The door was small and a part of a mighty oak tree in the forest. My lady approached the door cautiously. Austri opened the door before she could knock. He offered a place for my lady to rest for the night. In the morning, she received a beautiful green emerald to remind her of springtime. Freya mounted her chariot and her cats quickly pulled her towards the north.

As giant cats' paws pleasantly pattered the earth. The seasons changed as she journeyed across the vastness of the lands. Days turned to weeks, the weeks to months. The climate became hotter in the first few months.

It was the warm summer that came first. Then the leaves fell in autumn soon after. Finally came the snowy winter and the ice was everywhere once more. White as far as the eyes could see. Freya had lost the enjoyment of the chase again and the chill in the air began to bite. The frost had turned the greens to white and the world became a treacherous place to keep sure footing.

Her beautiful smile fell from her face. She became weary as her heart became sad once more. Her tears fell and the icy blizzards followed. The winds accelerated, sending shards of ice horizontal as they fell from the skies. It weighed heavier on my heart to see the one I loved hurt. "There is no hope in finding him. Our marriage and love are as dead and barren as this frozen wasteland," Freya wept.

Suddenly, a snowball hit her on the side. Her rage intensified as she curiously scanned her surroundings. Blinded by the blizzard, Freya heard a raven's call in the distance. The silhouette of a young boy with a wooden staff giggled at her. Freya shielded her eyes from the blizzard to decipher more of the young lad. He floated above the snow with white hair. "Come here, boy!"

The lad disappeared, running with ease through the thick and heavy snow. Freya pushed, wading through the snow.

As he faded from her sight, a colour appeared to her that made her recall the green grassy meadows. A dark green to contrast the white beyond the effects of winter. Her tears dried and the blizzard stopped. Making her way towards the colour, she found it was a wreath hanging from a door. She recalled the name I told her to go by in this region. Frau Holle named the wreath after herself as a hopeful welcome to weary winter travellers.

The holly bush would remain a symbol of love and understanding even through the darkest times. It would be a sign that love remained evergreen despite the harshness of the landscape. "Did you see him?" Norðri asked.

"The young boy? What do you know of him?"

"He goes by many names. A playful cold-loving boy. Where he goes, the frost usually follows. Jack Frost, he is known as throughout the lands."

Frau Holle was provided hospitality in Norðri's house and spent the night. Jack Frost made her realise that there can still be playful times in the harsh seasons. In the morning, she received a blue sapphire. It was a symbol of the winter season. Returning to her chariot, Freya rode south at a quicker pace. She realised I was Jack Frost, and I was close. Her cats pulled with haste as she longed to be reunited once more.

Freya travelled south through the spring and reached Egypt. Grass and mud were replaced by sand and dust. The freshness of spring faded as the heat from the summer sun brought her so much happiness.

As Bastet, Freya gifted these lands cats and in return, she became the mother goddess of the land of pharaohs. The cats were honoured and respected for their protection from rodent-fueled plagues around the people's grain stores. Life was good for all and even Freya enjoyed her solitude for a time.

Unfortunately, nothing lasts forever. From the ocean, Jormungandr slithered his way up the Nile. Under the name of Apophis, he wished to destroy the inhabitants where the rats failed. Jormungandr killed many cats, which gained my lady's attention. As Bastet, she held him at knifepoint and began to bargain for the people of the land. In exchange, Jormungandr desired a gift of the earth. He wanted the power of turning the mightiest of heroes to stone. However, Bastet told the serpent he would have to lay still while in the form of her choosing.

After the terms were agreed upon, Jormungandr left and during the celebrations, the dwarf Suðri appeared in the crowd and gave her a red ruby. This gemstone symbolised the joyous summertime when she bested the Midgard serpent for the good of the people and land.

She left the lands of Egypt in her cat-drawn carriage and headed west. Her pace was godly. The cats pulled her over the seas as quickly as the land. She admired her collection of gemstones as the wind made her red hair appear as fire trailing behind. Her beautiful green eyes, more precious than any stone, began to weep tears of joy. These tears were unlike any other as they dripped gold. I gathered as many of the tears as I followed her in secret.

Listen, good host, and listen well. If you should be lucky enough in love for a partner to cry for you. Hold on to those tears, in your mind and in your heart. Those tears are far more valuable than any trinkets of gold or silver in the short life you must endure.

When she landed in the country to the west, Freya was greeted immediately by the dwarf of Vestri. "Are you Coatlicue? Odin said you would show when the leaves fell from the trees. Here is a stone of amber. It represents when external beauty fades but life and beauty are more than outward appearance. Life itself is magnificent due to the seasons we experience. The highs, the lows, and it's the contradiction that gives us the understanding of both.".

Tired and spent, she rested at the dwarf's home. Freya had no clue what to do next or where to go. The following day before daybreak, I knocked on Vestri's door. I wasn't alone. I had gathered the other three dwarves and brought them to their brother's home.

"Greetings Vestri, son of the Brisings, I have gathered what I need for my gift. Here are the gold tears from my lady. I want you to send word for your brothers to gather. I require you to create the most beautiful necklace ever to exist. Each precious stone to be on show as a reminder that moods are like seasons, appreciate the beauty of contrast and the cycle of life they bring."

The four brothers spent three days in the burning and blazing forge. Clinking and clanking filled Vestri's home while we waited. At the end of the third day, the brothers carefully presented it to us. It was the most beautiful engagement gift of all time. They called it Brisingamen and it would give my lady the ability to control and understand the seasons. It was her earth, after all.

Ignorance vs Innocence

Freya and I departed from Vestri's home towards Midgard. We decided it was time for our sons to come home. We both glided amongst the clouds as falcons drifting through the skies freely. When we found our boys, we flew to a nest between them both. Their two kingdoms were at war and had been for decades. One desired power and the other fought for peace.

Geirrod plotted an attack from the south, while Sigurd and his forces defended their kingdom in the North. The battle was an epic stalemate with no clear victor in sight. Geirrod structured battle strategies that Sigurd quickly countered. Swords clashed, spears splintered and even axes became blunt after the many foes that fell. It was time for it to end and for our boys to come home to Asgard.

While my lady and I were perched high up in our nest, we decided to have another wager. This time the outcome of the battle. It didn't matter the outcome. The wars of men mean very little to gods. However, as long as our boys were assumed dead, they could return home.

"I will wager Sigurd's army will prevail, my lady."

"Geirrod's army has paid tribute to me, Odin. Can he not have the victory this time?"

"Very well, my lady. Whichever army exists in the North when I wake in three days shall have the victory and the glory that comes with it."

The wars of men come and go throughout history. They are merely a footnote in time and I only wished to show equality in my love and respect for my children. I had favoured Geirrod once before, and he had let me down. It was now Sigurd's turn to prove himself a worthy successor. He was noble in spirit and brave of heart but more importantly, he was a good king.

On the first day, I approached Geirrod. I was a weary old ambassador for Sigurd. I arranged for him to go west with a guard of similar build and look. I told him it was to witness his victory over Sigurd. A contest of single combat with the one that dethroned him so long ago. He was cautious of a trap because Sigurd still possessed the helmet of awe. I reassured him that his brother would fight fairly, that even the gods have ordained it.

"The gods will honour this fight with three gifts, good Geirrod. The gods have declared that you'll each have armour unlike any other to battle. You will learn your true names. The final gift is you will also be welcomed in Asgard," my voice echoed the skies above.

Geirrod stood back. He was both scared and intimidated, unsure if I was a mage of great power or Odin himself. I left a spark to ignite the desire for victory and glory in young Geirrod's heart. I departed his company with my sight on Sigurd.

The next day, I approached Sigurd's castle as his wise old uncle that had advised him before. It was under siege, so I took the secret entrance, behind the fireplace. He greeted me kindly, offering a meal and a seat to rest. "Uncle, do you require a clean cloth and a place to wash?" Sigurd respectfully asked.

"No, nephew, I am fine. I have travelled far because Skuld has told me it is time to come home."

"You're dying?" Sigurd's face showed concern.

"Not me but you, my boy. Odin and Freya request you to be present during their handfasting ceremony."

"But how? How do I get to Asgard?"

"There is an armour waiting for you in the west. It has a marking only visible to you and your rival. The marking is named Vegvisir. The Wayfinder, when worn on the head, will guide you to unknown shores even when you are lost. It will take you home, good king. Take one warrior of equal stature and form to end this rivalry with Geirrod finally."

After my meal, I exited the hall via the secret passage behind the fireplace. I returned to the nest where I would determine the war's outcome with my lady. At the same time, I was busy arranging our sons' return because she, too, had been busy. My Freya was cunning and tricky at her worst but nevertheless a master of disguise. She was the very personification of all that seduced, manipulated, and inspired. She was love and that defies knowledge. It can't be measured, explained, or defined. Love, beyond all, is the oasis in the desert.

During the night, as I slept, Freya entered Sigurd's castle. She approached his generals as the good king headed west to face his rival. Informing the generals of Geirrod's abandonment of his army, they became inspired to attack. Freya also disclosed that without their leader, the military would fall.

Once the army had left, she decided to execute the next part of her plan. She gained access to the slave quarters stealthily. She instructed the enslaved women in the castle to tie their long, luscious locks around the front of their chins as beards. Wearing whatever armour they could find, they had to use Geirrod's army's colours and dawn helmets to mask their beautiful features. Once her plan was cleverly complete, she departed the castle as a falcon from the southern wall.

Freya returned to the falcon nest as I slept. It was only a few moments later when Sol dragged the sun above the horizon. A new day dawned and rising from my slumber, I stretched. Yawning I looked to Sigurd's kingdom in the north. There were no soldiers on the wall and the army was nowhere in sight. Geirrod's army slew Sigurd's in the south, and with a blast of their horn, the victory echoed westward.

I could not be deceived so easily, but I allowed my lady her victory as there were more critical things to attend. Sure, it was dishonest of me to appear surprised by her victory but I love her. Wouldn't you allow your love a small victory that was insignificant of the bigger picture. A gift of superiority to the one I love. My failure for her happiness, love and respect seemed to be a fair trade to me.

Yule Tidings

After her victory, Freya and I left the nest and headed west. Both our boys were travelling with companions similar in stature and look. They wandered through the forests, slowly making their way toward each other. Geirrod was overly cocky since he had heard his army sound the victory horn. His servant of similar appearance offered him a drink to celebrate their army's victory over Sigurd. Those fools were blind to the challenge ahead. They were drunk with success and not respectful of the battle they were about to face.

Meanwhile, only a few kilometres away, Sigurd and his servant paid homage to the glorious dead that fought the noble fight. They died fighting for love. Love of their lands, homes and soldiers they fought beside. The warriors fought for freedom, family, and the fear of returning to the dictatorship of a king blinded by greed to the kingdom's needs.

Sigurd was the best kind of leader. Even in his youthfulness, he had surpassed me in so many different ways. He was everything I desired: humble, honourable, respectful, patient, kind, brave, adaptable, loving and strong. I was proud of the man he had become, though I would never be foolish enough to praise him so.

When he looked up from his respectful bow to the honoured dead, his eyes caught a glimpse of something. It was a brown fur coat shimmering like gold under the sun's embrace. He put it on, but something felt strange. The skin attached to his skin, he discovered power and comfort but could not pull the wolf's head over his as the helm of awe stopped it. He pulled his helmet off, handing it to his servant. As soon as he pulled the wolf's head over, he dropped to his knees.

Sigurd's skin burned hot as the coat twisted and engulfed his human form. Screams of pain turned to yelps and whimpers. The servant dropped the helmet of awe to tend to his king in his moment of despair. They both struggled as Sigurd's bones snapped and cracked. It was only moments but felt like a lifetime of pain to Sigurd. The wolf-skin stretched until there was no sight of human flesh.

The servant rushed for a blade to cut the skin off but it was too late. The noble Sigurd lost the essence of the man he once was. Many low growls became louder before the large wolf turned on his servant. Teeth, sharper than any sword, revealed themselves as saliva dripped from the beast's lower jaw.

The man slowly backed away, raising his shaky sword to his former king. The wolf bared its teeth as it stalked the man. Pouncing on the servant, the wolf claimed its prey. It mauled the man beyond recognition. When the servant's body is discovered, people will assume Sigurd fell. The unfortunate incident would be accepted as a wild attack by wolves in the woods.

Hodr's servant shared a similar fate after he discovered a similar skin. The day fell to darkness as the moon glowed in its full glory, and the embers of Muspelheim flickered and twinkled in the night. Geirrod and Sigurd howled as Mani pulled his charge across the dark skies. Those howls filled the valleys. It directed them toward each other as their claws trampled a pathway through the trees. Their paces quickened and their hearts raced as their rage overpowered their focus.

Suddenly, they came face to face with each other in a clearing. Teeth snapped, and wolves growled as each prepared to attack. The sound of falcons screeching in the skies above filled the silence. My lady and I dove down between our boys before they attacked each other. A bright light engulfed them both as I returned them to Ulfhednar form.

Still willing to fight as rivals, they continued to attack. Geirrod's fist met Sigurd's cheek and Sigurd delivered a powerful uppercut in return. They were so focussed on each other that they never realised they were in the presence of gods.

I threw off my cloak and transformed into a mighty beast. It was the power I gained from the mead of poetry and Loki's blood oath. It was a beast that would strike fear in most Jotun hearts. Bones broke and my flesh was shed. Half wolf and half-god, I was taller than them both. The sheer vision of my form caused the boys to stop their fight.

"Boys, your mother and I have decided it is time to come home. Don't fear me but you should always show respect in my presence. I am Odin, King of Asgard and, more importantly, your father."

"Odin, I would be happy to return to my kingdom victorious in battle. I thank you, Freya, for granting my army success on the battlefield," Geirrod bowed.

"Boy, you are unable to see the truth. Your name is not Geirrod; it is Hödr," I said as he stood back in amazement.

"The blind god of darkness and cold?" Hödr asked.

Sigurd was in awe but respectfully silent as Freya returned Hodr's godhood. A rush of wind and the shaking ground raised Geirrod from his feet. Vegvisir burned brightly on his forehead. His vision faded from him and he became panicked.

"Don't worry, boy, that magical emblem on your head will guide you, even if you cannot see."

My gaze then turned towards Sigurd. "Do you have any questions, loathe of Fafnir?"

"None Odin; I do not wish to waste your time with me. I will accept my defeat in the war and live out the remainder of my life as a humble wanderer," Sigurd said.

"That is why you will be my successor, boy. Your name is not Sigurd or Agnar, it is Baldur and your mother has missed you dearly."

Freya smiled at her son as he stepped back in awe. She revealed the helmet she had created so long ago. Freya had collected it from the area where Sigurd mauled his servant. The helmet of awe faded to golden glitter as the wind picked up and the earth shook. Sigurd elevated in the air as he emanated a blinding light.

The mark of Ægishjálmur appeared on his forehead as his godhood returned.

"Now hear me and hear me good loathe of Fafnir. You would be wise to apply my wisdom in your life. Do not remain awake at night unless to keep watch or to spy on another. Never fall asleep in a witch's arms, to never escape her warm embrace. Her magic will cloud your judgement and leave you lonely, with only her to provide comfort. Never confide in another's wife as they have proven themselves unfaithful. Be prepared when scaling the mountain of success. It has its hardships at the best of times without adding a lack of preparation. Never allow the ignorant knowledge of your misfortune. You will not receive comfort in your suffering. I've seen the words of a wicked heart wound a soul so profoundly that they lost their life. If you have a friend you trust, visit them often. The path of a good friendship must remain clear from foliage. Maintain a close friendship. It charms your life to have at least one. Never be hasty to destroy a close friendship. Sorrow will eat at you if you have no one to share thoughts with. Never waste words of wisdom with a fool. You will never gain a good return. Sharing wisdom with the honourable will assure you of his favour through praise. The true meaning of friendship is honesty, brutality included. Those that only say nice things are unreliable. Do not waste effort on a worthless fight. There is strength in walking away. Be comfortable and steady on your own path before giving advice. If you are not, it will only bring uncertainty and doubt to your wisdom. If you see wrong, call it what it is. To allow it is to encourage your enemies. Never smile in victories of lies and deceit. Instead, take pleasure in honourable success. When you rule, never let the mortals look to you for victory. Men can become mad when they believe they have the support of higher powers. If you wish to court a good woman, make beautiful promises and keep them, a man is only as good as his word. It is wise to be cautious of alcohol and another's wife and a thief trying to deceive you. Never allow disrespect from a guest or even a wanderer. Never trust those claiming perfection or utter failure. None are without blemish or made useless by their failure. Never mock the old if they decide to share wisdom. Their grey hair and wrinkles are marks of wisdom in a long journey of life and hardship. Never chase guests away. Remain hospitable until their actions dictate their own departure. When you receive Draupnir, be sure to gift your guests. They will be less likely to curse you if you increase their wealth and respect their presence. If you choose to drink, remain grounded. A drunken celebration can leave you vulnerable to an attack from inside your home, sickness or even the spells of a witch," I said to guide Baldur when he claimed the throne to become king of Asgard.

"Make your way home, my sons. One will guide, the other will protect, and we will celebrate your return on the day I wed your father," Freya's beautiful and wise words echoed on the wind. I shrunk back down to my form as an old man, as my cloak levitated and returned to my shoulders. Nothing more was said. I smiled, letting my sons know I was happy to see them in their actual forms. Freya and I returned to our falcon forms before flying north, toward Asgard.

The Nutcracker

It was summertime in Asgard when Hödr and Baldur finally found their way home. Life was great and the Jotun race remained peaceful for the most part. The birds rejoiced and sang a beautiful melody that you would have thought they had drunk from the mead of poetry. Even the haunting calls of ravens and crows ceased for a time out of joy for Baldur, the beautiful's return with his mighty blind brother.

Sol dragged the glorious day slower, prolonging the Joy as Freyr prepared for the celebrations of Sigurblòt. It was a feast for summer to celebrate the beginning of the good days when the weather is in your favour. Festivities that brought people together around a boar on a spit. This was Freyr's attempt to woo Sol, a love that will forever be out of his reach.

The summer joys widened my lady's delicate and luscious lips, which warms my heart to witness. I was preparing to make the most honourable oaths a man and woman could make to each other. I was ready to bind our hands and hearts in a handfasting ceremony. The summer was made more beautiful with the embrace of her glowing expression that rivalled the beauty of Brisingamen.

Every hardship I had endured up to this day had washed away, absorbed by Muninn. I was happy in the present and that is why gifting is so important today. The joy you receive in the exchange of the happiness you gift when you give people presents, good host. Whether it is the insight of wisdom, an empathetic ear, or your heart, simply knowing there is someone offering kinship to help fight the battles of life. Whether it's a war against enemies or the ones not visible to the naked eye, your presence is more important in the present than any object.

The gods gathered on the mound as my lady and I stood upon the highest peak of the ground where our ancestors were laid. All could see our union of love and learning. They journey together in life for the good of our children. The ones that stood and watched us, the ones on Midgard that we inspire and my father, Bor and his father before him had been laid to rest.

When it comes to love, your thoughts should always be directed towards whatever your heart desires. That is the bigger picture. Your life affects those around you and your heart is the engine that drives you to your hopes and dreams. Sometimes the choice begins as yours and sometimes the Norns force your evolution through time. Learn from the past, live in the present and love all the possibilities the future holds.

The time for our ceremony was high noon and it was finally time to make our oaths to each other. Lofn led the ceremony in her noble duties. The crowd smiled as we took our commitments. Muninn sat on my shoulder while Huginn, I thought, was away scouting the realms collecting information.

I looked deep into her loving eyes. Both sparkled in the sunlight. Gersemi and Gnoss smiled back at me, greener than the hillside meadows. A single golden tear ran down from the windows of her soul. I used my thumb to gently wipe her tear away as I felt more prosperous than ever.

"My love, anywhere you go, I promise to follow. If I can, I will counsel as a good wife should. There will be times I need your warmth to help me back from a cold dark winter's night. I want to share our springs and our summers and when the dark times approach, we will be there to support each other. I love you, Odin, that I promise never to love another," Freya told me, gently holding my hand.

My heart swelled as I gathered myself to make my oath. "I will love you in this life and the next until I enter the jaws of Fenrir. I swear to ease your burdens so that others can appreciate your splendour. When times appear at their darkest and hope begins to dwindle, my love will seek you. My heart will be bonded to yours. You will be my Freya to others but my beloved, my Frigg, to me. I don't want the world to see me as you do. I don't think that they'll understand. Nothing lasts forever, love included. We can only appreciate the magic it brings when we have it to hold. I only want you to know who I truly am. I love you, Frigg and if I lose you, I will find you again."

We sealed the moment with a kiss and our Wyrd was forever intertwined as we swore on Gungnir. She was my guiding light on the horizon of my mind. Frigg was my thought guiding me like a compass toward the future. The union enriched all the lands below the Skylands. Midgard flourished, the forests of Svartalfheim glimmered in the shadows and even the coldest, darkest cave in Jotunheim brightened a little.

Suddenly, an unusual freeze filled the air as the sky darkened. An icy chill in the summer meant something was seriously wrong. It was like Ragnarok had come early. The sun disappeared behind a black cloud, like it had been swallowed by the wolf that pursued. The grass turned black without Sol's light gracing us. I searched my love's face for answers, but she was unsure too. I looked toward my brother Heimdall and asked what he could see.

"A blizzard beyond Asgard's walls. An army of yeti preparing for war," Heimdall strained his eyes to see beyond the snow and mist. "I can't make it out fully, but a witch is causing this frightful winter. Careful, Odin, she looks powerful."

"Verdandi," I mumbled to myself. "Thor, Tyr, Baldur! Are you ready to fight? Let us go to war together!" I roared like a mighty lion.

The gates of Asgard opened slowly, revealing tens of thousands of yetis snarling and growling with ferocity. Each of them, with weapons raised, were eager to taste the blood of gods. Clubs and axes raised high, waiting for the witch's orders that led them.

I turned to my boys, proud to be fighting by their side, but I never spoke of it. The burden of a father is to praise but not too much too soon. I just smiled from the corner of my mouth and nodded toward them all.

Thor stood tall on his goat-drawn carriage with teeth clenched and bared and Mjolnir raised high. The Thunder rolled in with the lightning cracking in the sky. Tyr looked noble on his mighty horse. His reins were attached to his stump and his sword pointed toward the enemy. Baldur sat upon Magni's horse Gulfaxi with his glow reflected in the horse's golden mane.

I turned toward the enemy and my grip tightened on Gungnir. My nightmarish stallion grunted and scraped the ground with its front four legs. It was hungry and could be tempered with the flesh of many Jotuns. "Boys! These Jotun seem to be eager for death! Let's end their appetites with their own! I swear by Gungnir that no god dies today. Leave the witch to me. For Asgard!" I yelled as the eight-legged Kelpie drew my sleigh. My sons followed behind as the witch signalled the yeti to attack.

The yeti's march shook the skies. The mortals below cowered as the cold winter had gripped the world below. The sounds of war high above were only drowned out by the goats of Thor, rumbling across the skies. Flashes of light illuminated the world only for random spurts before the darkness returned.

As the battle ensued above, the yeti fell quickly. Each hammer blow marked as a lightning strike as Thor slew many. Tyr returned to his giant monstrous bear form, slashing his enemies rapidly. Baldur was immune to harm, so each attack they attempted failed. He smiled at his enemy before beating them with his bare hands.

As Sleipnir slid through hundreds of yetis toward the witch, her appearance became more apparent the closer I came. It wasn't Verdandi but someone that had crossed my path before. "Gunlodd, call off your assault!" I screamed over the deafening winds.

"She died long ago, Odin. I am Skadi now and I have a come to claim the death debt of my father."

"Skadi, how did you get here? Today was supposed to be a celebration and enough have died today," I said as Thor and Tyr gathered at my side, ready to attack. She smiled at us condescendingly. Thor raised his hammer as he rushed at her. Skadi swept his legs away, grounding his attempt and ending it with a mighty blow to Thor's face, sending him unconscious. She raised her bow and directed it at my bear son.

"Bears are easy to hunt. Big targets," she said, drawing her bow back. I immediately deflected the arrow and saved my son from instant death. However, she now had me in her sights. She released the arrow and it flew toward me. I closed my eyes as my thoughts took me to my love's embrace. Fond memories of a life lived but then I remembered my fate. No wolf was near as Fenrir remained in his chains. I opened my eyes to a bright glow in front of me.

"Baldur, my love," Skadi said in awe.

"Skadi, you can't kill me and I won't allow you to hurt my family. There must be another way we can settle this to avoid any more bloodshed," Baldur said, making her stern look ease slightly.

"I haven't smiled since before my father's death. I am alone in pain and require something to remember my father by."

"What if we gods guarantee you will smile again. We will give you a husband of your choosing and, with it, a land named after you and your chosen husband. My love and I will gift you a jewel to remember your father and the knowledge he has been guiding you from afar. Come to my hall. We shall fulfill your wishes," I said as her gaze remained fixed on Baldur. The blizzard cleared and the sun was restored to its glory. The birds sang as Baldur triumphed in battle, and my horse of death feasted on the countless corpses scattered over the battlefield.

We returned to my hall beyond Asgard's wall, where the Sigurblòt restarted. We were careful where we stepped. The thousands of dead yetis were treated as the honourable dead should. All remained respectful and honourable between the guest and the hosts. The feasting table was packed, and our bellies were empty. It is always better to make peace on a full stomach than the desperation that comes with an empty one.

I sent an elf for Loki to take charge of the feast's entertainment. After cracking a few jokes that displeased Skadi, she began to sniff his scent. "You! I've smelled you before! It was Loki that stole my charge, my responsibility! You think you are the greatest of all time, with your humour, your trickery, and your magic. I bet you can't even beat one of Thor's goats in a test of strength," Skadi glared.

"You are a bit nutty, aren't you?" Loki smirked.

"Nutty? Yes, you valued your nuts when you were that squirrel stealing from me. Tie one end of the rope to the goat's beard and the other to Loki's balls."

The room was silent as all looked towards Loki as he nervously gulped in fear. I wasn't pleased with this as he was under my protection by a blood oath. I tried to sway her decision but Skadi was humiliated. I had hurt her heart and Loki had damaged her pride.

Thor secured the rope to Tanngrisnir's beard while I regretfully handed the other end to Loki. Loki turned from us, lifting his shirt and tying the rope down his pants. He winced and flinched as the rope was tightened.

And then it began. The goat bleated and pulled as Loki squealed out in agony. Loki uncomfortably pulled back, providing temporary relief until the rope tightened again. My hall was filled with laughter and suffering. This went back and forth while Skadi's stern look became a smirk. Suddenly the rope snapped and Loki collapsed in imaginable pain on Skadi's lap.

The room burst into booming laughter. Only two remained silent. Frigg and I took no pleasure in the disgrace of one of our own. I helped Loki to his feet while calling for Eir's skills. Thor's bellowing laughs got the better of him when he decided to mock Loki. "Fond of horses, Loki, but it takes a goat to make your weapon limp." That comment would come back to bite him one day.

As the laughter died, it was time for the following promise of peace. "Now your mood is better. It is time to select a husband.".

"I choose Baldur!" Skadi shouted eagerly.

"Not so fast, my girl. You like games, how about we play one of my own. You can select your husband but only by looking at his feet.".

The gods gathered behind a curtain with only their feet on show. It felt like an age ago when I constructed this. When she was Gunlodd, I used Njord's feet as part of my disguise as they remained beautifully unaffected by years of wandering that both Baldur and I had endured.

Skadi paced up and down as her gaze and instincts drew her toward two sets of feet. One looked perfectly presented with no signs of imperfections. The other looked nice but had signs of being well used. "I choose those feet. Nothing on my beloved could ever be imperfect," Skadi proclaimed. Much to her disappointment, when the curtain was unveiled, the owner of the feet was Njord.

It goes to show good host. Loving someone due to their apparent perfection is foolish. The future will reveal the truth in time. A beautiful heart will always outlive an attractive appearance. See a heart and know a mind. If you judge the surface, you will forever be blind.

After nine nights in Jotunheim amongst the mountainous landscapes and cold weather, the wolves howled. Njord was very uncomfortable with his new wife's home. The haunting howls echoed amongst the wind's whistles. Wendigos growled and snarled, fighting over scraps of an unlucky animal. Njord's mind was on his wife and marriage, but his heart was on the sea.

Compromise doesn't always work when it comes to love. Be true to your heart and your mind will be at peace.

After nine nights in Nóatún, Skadi became unsettled. The calming effects of the waves in the silence of the night made her uneasy. The gentle rocking of boats to and fro, like a baby's crib, wasn't for her. What is suitable for one isn't always good for the other. Life and love are about growth and adaptation. Be aware of love's wisdom but enjoy the triumph you face together.

She followed the north star back to Asgard for her final request for peace. "Odin, I have come to request a keepsake to remember my father's death."

"You have travelled the same path as him. He has guided you here. He was my enemy, but I gifted him great power as a Phoenix high above us.

That north star is your father watching over us as a guiding light to navigate our freedom in this complicated world."

I plucked Suttung's eye from my head, handing it to Frigg. She clasped her hands tightly with it in between. As she slowly revealed what now was beneath, a tear ran down Skadi's cheek.

"Take this diamond, sister. It will remind you that Suttung still twinkles like a diamond in the sky. Hold it close to your heart and remember him. That is all you need, warrior queen," Frigg said softly.

"My Frigg has made a collection of countries in the north of Midgard in honour of your union to Njord. A home by the sea and beautiful mountains filled with animals to hunt. Scandinavia is the perfect combination for you both. I hope your love of the land will blossom in your marriage," I said, keeping my promises to the mighty warrior.

"Odin, Verdandi sent me to kill you and leave Asgard in ruins. I fear she'll set her sights on Baldur now he is home.".

"Thank you, Skadi. It honours me to have you on my side," I said, retiring to my throne to plot the following defence of peace against the Norn witch of Jotunheim.

Responsibility vs Intelligence

Six months had passed since peace was made with Skadi. It was a still and calm night as all slept, all except one. The breeze in Asgard gently flew through the open windows of my bed chambers. Loki stewed for months, feeling humiliated like never before. Unaware of my deception of Skadi as a result of his mistreatment, he became poisonous of thought and intent towards his own kin. He was left hurting by the shame of not only his physical wounds but the emotional ones too.

As Frigg and I slumbered beneath the sheets, something small drifted lightly on the wind. A faint buzz quietly filled the room as a fly drifted around the room. The quiet returned as Loki found the bedside table. It was where my Frigg would always place her beautiful necklace, Brisingamen.

As Sol dragged the sun over the horizon, it dawned on my beloved that her necklace was gone. As I looked into the precious treasure that was her beautiful green eyes, I was bewitched, unable to speak. I had enough and there is wisdom in knowing that, good host. I brushed her beautiful red hair from her cheek only to smile like any gullible fool entranced by love. She subtly smiled from the corner of her mouth as she looked back at me. Then words trickled from her lips gently. "I have to go, my love."

The beauty of anything is in the understanding of the contrast. How can you appreciate someone's presence if they never go? How can you appreciate relaxation if you don't work hard? How can someone truly know joy without experiencing the lows that sorrow brings? How can someone understand life if they never die? That is why it is better to be a middle wise, good host. Everything has to end to appreciate the precious time you have to experience.

Frigg left concerned about my reaction to the loss of my engagement gift. She went directly to her best option for recovering such an elegant artefact. She used her feathered cloak to soar amongst the Skylands of Asgard. She drifted, in falcon form, to Himimbjörg, where she landed in a panic. "Heimdall! Heimdall! I need your aid!"

"What do you require of me, Jord, my queen?"

"Brisingamen is missing! I must have it back. Please can you locate it for me?"

"I shall return it to you, my queen. You have my oath. Go back to Odin and tell him the truth. He will appreciate the honesty."

Heimdall stood at the edge of the Bifrost for a year, looking for clues to the necklace's location. After a year of scanning every millimetre of land coming up fruitless, he turned his gaze to the oceans. As he stared a little harder to access the underwater world that once belonged to the Vanir, he became entranced.

It was beautiful, the open water realm with spectacular shades of blue that eventually faded to black. Straining his eyes, he searched the darkness. There wasn't much down there. Only Aegir and Ran, with their collection of dead servants collected by the cruel sea. Peering further, there he was, the world serpent sleeping soundly, sucking on its tail in peace.

Heimdall was amazed at such a world of wonder. This world was full of luminescent fish and coral, enormous whales and fish with razor-sharp teeth. Eight-legged giant octopuses grabbing their prey and consuming the dead fish. The oceans of Vanaheim have their beauty but they also have their dangers.

Heimdall spent an entire year searching the ocean's secrets only to discover Loki existing as a Selkie. A male seal skinned creature that preyed on the heartbroken maidens dripping tears into the water from the coastline. It summoned Loki from the depths to seduce these women and lead them into the water with the promise of revenge on males. Using his twisted version of Seidr magic, he created Sirens from his greedy nature to twist sadness into monstrous things.

These Sirens were half fish and half beautiful maiden and were created for one purpose. It was to destroy those brave seafarers by toying with their hearts and minds. Those Sirens would lure males with a beautiful voice filled with enchanting words and a glamourous appearance on the surface, masking the monstrous nature beneath the waves. They would glide amongst the currents, seductively alluring their victims to drown and consume them in the depths of depression, where they would be left to sink in the cold dark abyss of the unexplored ocean.

Heimdall grasped his sword, called Hed, tightly before leaving his post. He journeyed over the rainbow bridge and across the land to the coastline at the edge of Midgard, missing Loki by moments on land.

Loki's seal form appeared above the water's surface to smirk at Heimdall's failure. Heimdall used his head and extraordinary abilities to look and listen far and wide. The day proved to be fruitless but when Mani dragged the full moon over the sky, he heard a commotion.

It was a lover's quarrel, but it was the words spoken that caused his attention. "Please give it back. It is mine and my freedom. It was my skin and I wish to join my sisters and play carefree amongst the waves. I'm a free spirit that doesn't wish to be chained in the shackles of marriage. You don't want a wife with a heart that belongs to the sea, do you?"

"You were a Selkie, but your beauty belongs to me now. And you will give me many beautiful children."

Heimdall's pace quickened. Each footstep shook the ground until he reached the arguing couple. "This skin you speak of, what is it?" he asked the pair.

"You have gold teeth?" the man asked while being awestruck. Before allowing Heimdall to answer, he grabbed the lady's arm to keep her silent. "This is my lady, and her skin belongs to me. She'll learn to love me more than her precious sea and freedom."

"Give me the skin, you petty little man. I need it to return something precious to the goddess of love."

"No, you can't..." with a swing of his mighty blade, the man's life was no more.

"Lady, allow me to use your skin to recover what was lost and you have my word I will return it to you."

The lady smiled and agreed as she knew Heimdall would keep his oath. She recognised Heimdall from his description in legends passed down and if anyone were loyal to their word, it would be the golden toothed god that watches over the lands. He was the god that remained vigilant and observant of all severe threats to gods and mortals alike.

Heimdall wore the sealskin and transformed into a Selkie just as Loki did. He swam beneath the water and began his search. The magic of the seal skin enhanced his vision further. He could see the sharks sniffing the scent of blood in the water. He could see the coral illuminating the darkness and then he saw Loki carrying Brisingamen in his jaws. He flew at an incredible pace through the ocean, creating underwater currents not visible to the human eye.

Although the surface remained unaffected, the turbulence of Heimdall's pursuit of Loki was something quite epic. The water behind was cyclonic, generating a vacuum where no water creature could exist. The sudden impact created a massive air bubble killing the Sirens nearby.

Each of them returned to human form to battle each other. Blow after mighty blow but the match remained even until Heimdall drew his sword and used his head to strike at the heart of Loki's character. "I don't mind a challenge from my offspring, but I refuse to believe that your nature is so damaged that you would steal from your own mother.".

Loki paused for an instant to reflect on his actions. A moment that allowed Heimdall to strike and with a blow to the leg, Loki released Brisingamen and as it floated below the air pocket, Heimdall returned to seal form. He swam swiftly to collect his prize.

On his way back to Frigg, battered and bruised, he returned the sealskin to the lady. She was free again to join her sisters in the waves during the day and dance in the moonlight amongst the darkness. The Selkies were free-spirited woman folk that enjoyed their frolicking amongst the waves. The lady was given her life back once more thanks to the noble Heimdall. He continued to limp toward a secluded area far from mortal eyes. He summoned the Bifrost and returned the necklace to its rightful owner.

Eir tended to his wounds on his arrival to Himinbjörg and I watched Loki drifting beneath the waves upon my throne. It was heartbreaking to observe not only my stepchild but a friend suffer from depressive overthinking. His mind was turbulent and his heart withered. Loki plotted his next act of chaotic mischief beneath the tides.

Beware the Krampus

Months had passed since Loki's defeat to Heimdall, and it was time I brought him back to the table. I sent word to every realm that the gods needed to gather. Word was sent to the dwarven realm for Frigg to attend. A Valkyrie was sent to Scandinavia for Skadi and Njord to attend. I requested Thor and Sif's attendance also. Freyr, Heimdall, Tyr and Sigyn, Idunn and Bragi and finally, I used Sleipnir to travel over the ocean's surface above Vanaheim and pull Loki from the depths. I wrapped him in a warm blanket and proceeded to Valhöll. Prancer, the monstrous Kelpie, dragged the sleigh over the water, up the mountains and into the sky.

Frigg prepared the meal for the feast. Her cooking was an enchanted form of her witchcraft, with the ability to transform poisonous food from terrible texture and taste to nourishment full of flavour. That's witchcraft at its finest. Remember that food fuels the body and feeds the soul. The magic is in the skill of the craft and the balance of the combination of flavours. Take it too far and the magic is lost.

Everyone had a place to sit. Baldur was with Nanna, amusing their child called Forseti. Hödr waited patiently for all to arrive as the guests took their seats. I called for silence in the rowdy room. There will be a time for pleasantries, but the purpose of this feast was to inform every god of my decision on a successor. I know this would create friction in the family, but the honourable path is long and straight.

"I have gathered each of the gods here today to declare who will lead you when I am gone. I know some are great fighters and others have suffered for victory in the name of Asgard. Some are noble in upholding peace through justice, and some are responsible for looking after the nine realms. Noble Freyr, you govern the magical elves providing beautiful solutions to nature's wonders but remain focused on your pursuit of a loving partner. Hödr, I taught you how to rule but not the why. My decision is Baldur."

I quietly watched the reaction of those at the table. Freyr huffed as he rose from his chair to depart the hall. I knew where he was going and I would deal with that accordingly. Thor's knuckles became white with frustration and Loki's jaw clenched furiously with the announcement of Baldur's rule. "Thor and Loki walk with me to the arena," I said, hoping to keep the peace at the table.

We strolled while each of them pleaded their case. I said nothing until we were all standing in the centre. "Thor, your arrogance is your weakness. Hrungnir's whetstone still affects your judgement and when you combine, your lack of failure makes you an unwise choice for leadership." Thor's grip tightened on Mjolnir as the thunder rolled in. Loki remained quiet as he backed away from the fight.

Before Thor began his challenge, I pointed Gungnir toward Loki. "Loki, your thirst for revenge and enjoyment of chaos makes you unworthy of the throne. You are quick to wrath and your judgement is poor. You are a talented liar, making you a great politician but not a great leader. The only way you'll be king is over my corpse."

The skies became dark as the arena rumbled. Flashes of light revealed Thor's growing angry expression. The Skylands wept as father faced son again. I took a deep breath before assuming my battle position. Thor raised his hammer and lightning hit it, charging the mighty weapon for a life-ending blow. I swiftly swept his legs underneath him, sending him parallel to the ground. I magically transformed Thor's angry expression into a look of shock as I grabbed his armour at the chest and slammed him to the ground.

Unable to rise, the dark clouds dispersed, and clarity returned to the mighty hero. "Your might and strength do not dictate your ability to rule. True strength lies in the ability to control," I said, helping him reach his feet. "You know how to fight but do not know how to accept that there is no defeat if one walks away. You and Loki must travel to Utgard in Jotunheim. Seek out the king there and perhaps you may learn something."

Both mounted Thor's chariot and descended into Midgard. Thunder trembled in the clear skies as Tanngrisnir and Tanngnjóstr galloped amongst the clouds. Thor found calm while travelling to a farm on the edge of Jotunheim. It was as if working the lands helped him honour his mother, and there was peace in that. Fields of grain on a warm summer's day allow one to work hard for the good of the people. There is more than one way to aid the people of Midgard.

With a flash of light, Thor, Loki and his goats arrived safely at the small farm. Thor secured his goats to a pine tree just outside the home. Both strolled toward the door with the hard ground and grass crunching underneath each step. It took three firm knocks before the door gave way and revealed who was inside to the thunderer. There was a mother and father with two children. The boy and girl cowered as soon as the door opened.

The boy, called Thyalfi, hid under the table. At the same time, the little girl, Röskva, remained quiet behind her father's chair. "Relax, good farmers. We have come to seek hospitality before continuing to Jotunheim. We will even provide the meat for a feast to honour your hospitality. All I ask is that you leave the bones intact," Thor spoke softly to appear less threatening. Slowly, the people revealed themselves from their hiding places. "Ha ha ha, good people thank you for your aid on our journey," Thor bellowed. All was jolly as he welcomed the parents with a handshake and hugs. The little boy and girl were eager to hear Thor's stories while sitting in the oversized chair.

Suddenly, the door opened again to reveal a horned silhouette and monstrous form. A creature from the darkest of horrors the mind could conjure. It was like a Satyr but more nightmarish. Its teeth were as sharp as a crooked shark's smile. "Can I eat them," hissed the creature at the door.

"Loki enough! You are scaring them!" Thor's booming voice trembled the house. Even the inhabitants of Jotunheim could feel the rumbles. Loki morphed from his demonic Krampus form to his standard shape, becoming more pleasant to ease the farmer and his family. "Relax, I was jussst having fun."

"If you think that's fun, perhaps I should tell these lovely folk about the time my goat defeated you," Thor said sternly.

Loki's smirk fell from his face. He began plotting revenge on Thor and the goat that shamed him. Loki was sly and he would have his victory over Thor. His triumph would result in something I would need. Thor shared many tales with the residents, stories of battle and glory. However, the day was getting late and it was time for dinner.

Thor stood up from his chair and exited the door, making his way toward his goats. Gathering wood into a pile, he constructed a spit. The kind used to roast meat. Using Mjolnir, he summoned lightning strikes to end his goats' lives. "Loki!" Thor called out.

"Yesss, Thor, what do you need?"

"Do you still have the ability of fire you absorbed from Mimir's ring?"

"Yesss, I'll just grab some dry leaves to fuel the fire."

After placing them on the fire, he tapped into his Geri side. I thought it was buried deep, but perhaps his shame was the fuel his dormant side required. His eyes went from green to red as his hands conjured an ember first, then a flame. Quickly, it spread like wildfire throughout the pile of sticks. Thor thanked him and began cooking the meat to feed the hosts.

With the magical fire, it wasn't long before the meat was cooked through. Everyone sat down to a succulent feast prepared by Thor. Each of them had enough to fill their bellies three times over. As each had their fill, Thor reminded them to stack the bones on the pelts under the tree outside, undamaged and intact. Loki inhaled a single portion and retired to his bed. Each family member was satisfied with one amount, too, before retiring to slumber at night.

All on his own, Thor laughed to himself as he devoured everyone's extra portions as the evening drifted into night. His belly swelled as he finished his last bite before passing out on the huge chair. The fire flickered until the flames dwindled. A low grumbly snore echoed throughout the house.

Perhaps this part of the legend is the source of the jolly fat man I'm thought to be in modern times.

A Gift Under the Tree

In the dead of night, when all slept, something stirred in the shadows—lurking, in wait, until the night was at its darkest. Just before dawn, Loki decided to have what he considered fun. As the Krampus, he crept into the children's room. Quiet like a rat or a sinister serpent. He sneaked across the floor, slithering until he reached the bottom of Thyalfi's bed.

Loki began to hiss incantations as his haunting eyes burned dark red. Thyalfi began to stir as nightmarish illusions entered his dreams. His body became restless as the cold sweats caused him to shiver. Loki's eyes lit up the room as Thyalfi's dreams intensified and he began to mumble. Thyalfi could not wake of his own accord due to Loki's magical manipulation.

As his mumbles became groans and Röskva woke in her bed across the room. She witnessed Loki in Krampus form tormenting her brother. Bravely, she launched her pillow at the hideous creature's head. Interrupting his spell, she called out to her brother. "THYALFI! RUN!".

Suddenly, Thyalfi's eyes widened to reveal the creature at the bottom of the bed. He charged courageously toward the monster knocking him over with his incredible speed. Grabbing his sister's arm, they retreated through the door. They ran past Thor while he slept heavily. The children's screams of panic never woke any adult lying in the house. It was almost as if Loki had enchanted their sleep to ensure it.

Both burst from the house as the light showed on the horizon. Loki pursued with his mouth salivating, eager to taste their young flesh. A single Raven called out as it stood by the goats' bones under the tree. Hesitantly the two children grabbed the bones, snapping the leg. Each took either end of the bone, sucking out the marrow.

Loki burst from the residence and charged at them both. However, with the magical marrow, Thyalfi roared as his shape grew larger. "NO!" fur replaced skin as he broke free from the restraints of his clothes. Loki fell back in fear as Thyalfi became a berserker. A giant bear with the strength of nine grown men. Massive claws and teeth, eyes as dark as night, bared at Loki.

Regaining his footing, Loki attempted to grab Röskva on his right side. She looked up toward him, unafraid. Grabbing his ankle, she began swinging his body high above her head, like a ragdoll. Giggling innocently, the girl started slamming his limp body to the ground repeatedly until he was in an open grave.

The night turned to day as Thor woke from his slumber. He stretched, unaware of Loki's mischief during the night. Exiting the house, he finds something extraordinary in the morning. Thyalfi was naked and Röskva was looking down at a hole in the ground. He told Thyalfi to go inside and get clothed as he approached the hole. He peered down to find Loki battered, bruised, and gasping for air. "Did you have a good rest, Loki?" Thor smiled.

"I have had better!"

Thor grew tired of the games and walked toward the bones and skins of his goats. I flapped my black wings and took off to observe from above. Thor threw Mjolnir above the remains. The clouds darkened as he mumbled the magical phrase. With a blinding flash of light, the hammer restored the goats to life. Instantly noticing Tanngrisnir's limp leg, Thor's rage grew. The sky raged above as he threatened to destroy the home and all who reside there.

As Loki emerged to witness Thor slipping into an arrogant rage, he smirked. Verdandi's curse imbued into Hrungnir's whetstone made Thor lose his nobility in the moment. A mighty warrior made impatient and arrogant has no honour and no right to become king.

Just then, Thyalfi stood at the doorway. Thor recognised someone familiar, but it wasn't the boy he sent to get clothed. The giant bear roared in defiance of Thor. The thunderer paused to gather himself while the raven's call from above made him think. He thought of Tyr's sacrifice to control the angry Fenrir, realising he was becoming no better than the beast imprisoned by Gleipnir.

The dark and stormy clouds cleared as Thor's temper faded. The parents offered to take care of the goats during Tanngrisnir's recovery. Thyalfi returned to his boy form once more only to quickly offer his services of aid. Thor pondered the difficult journey ahead without his goats to aid him and agreed. "Röskva, you will be coming too. Odin will know what to do with your newfound abilities."

Packing only what they could carry, they continued with limited supplies searching for the mysterious Utgard Loki's castle. All left the farm in search of answers and wisdom. None realised that before this journey was over, they could never return to their old lives again.

He Sees You When You're Sleeping

All four travellers went high up the mountains and over the lands. The sun became intense, and the heat was warmer than the usual climate of Jotunheim. They walked for miles and just as the sun rested on the horizon, they found shelter in an abandoned cave. They set up camp and everyone slept silently.

It was a peaceful night and no creature stirred. All was silent as the temperature dropped, causing the flickering flame of the campfire to dwindle. The stillness of the night was replaced with a strange rumbling of the earth. Not enough to cause a panic but enough to be mildly irritating to some of the travellers.

The rumbles woke the mighty Thor first. He stood up and tightened Megingjord. He pulled his Jarngreipirs on before grabbing Mjolnir and headed out of the cave. The closer he came to the entrance, the noise became louder, and the earthquakes became a little more vigorous.

While emerging from the shelter, the shaking ground intensified even further. As Thor investigated the source, his mind began to search for possibilities. Was it a herd of giant Oxen or Buffalo? Was it his great goats on their way to aid them in their journey? Or was it my Frigg concerned about her boys' well-being?

Thor's brain scrambled for answers, and his eyes began deciphering what he could see. Sol created the dawn while Thor rubbed his eyes in disbelief. A giant of immense size lay sleeping not far from the cave. The giant was a dwarf compared to Ymir but at least three times larger than Hrungnir. This titan began to wake as Thor stood in awe at this being's colossal size.

The giant yawned and stretched as he began to search for something. "Ah, little person. Have you seen a glove by any chance?" the giant said pleasantly. Thor couldn't talk as he couldn't believe what he was seeing. "Speak, little one. Ah, it doesn't matter. There it is." The giant reached toward the cave everyone sheltered in. Grabbing the glove, Loki and the children fell outside of their shelter. What they thought was a cave was, in fact, the sleepy giant's glove. "I am Scyrmir, little folk, and if I'm not mistaken, you are Thor, and you are Loki. I am a little confused about who the others are," the giant scratched his head.

"We are Thyalfi and Röskva, giant! Can you help us find a castle in these lands, please!" Thyalfi yelled courageously.

"Maybe that's who you were but your true names have yet to be discovered. I'm heading toward a castle. If you want to meet Utgard Loki, I can carry your rations if you'd like?"

Thor eagerly agreed, foolishly handing over his food and other supplies. A good leader never burdens another with a load they can bear themselves. Skyrmir placed everyone's supplies into his massive bag before sealing it shut with an unusual iron wire. Loki should have recognised the wire. He had an experience long ago with it due to an oath not being upheld.

They travelled from sunrise to sunset. Each giant step forced the rest to run to keep up. Panting and exhausted, the travellers caught up to Skyrmir who was already set up for his rest. "That'll do for today, little gods. Your supplies are in my bag. Help yourselves. I'm exhausted and here looks as good a place as any for a good sleep," yawned Skyrmir just before drifting into a deep slumber.

The Aesir and the children gasped, trying to catch their breath. Collecting themselves, Thor offered to cook a feast for everyone. Climbing up the giant's bag, he reached the opening. He pulled and he tugged, he heaved, and he shrugged. The bag wasn't opening. That iron wire that sealed it was not budging, not even a little. It didn't matter how strong he was; he should never have relied on another to control what sustained them.

After struggling for an hour, Loki and the children decide to rest and wait till morning for a meal. However, Thor became angry with hunger as time waned on into the night. While the others slept, Thor grabbed his hammer with his stomach growling. He didn't want to kill the giant. He just wanted to wake him.

Thor scaled the giant's face until he found himself on Skyrmir's forehead. He gently tapped the snoring giant and a tiny lightning spark struck the giant as the hammer made contact. The giant giggled in his sleep. Dismissing the blow as part of a dream, Skyrmir continued to snore in his slumber. Thor decided to be patient like the others and try to sleep until morning.

As the night continued, Thor became more restless with hunger and starvation. He raised Mjolnir halfway as the grey clouds rolled in overhead. Bringing the hammer down a little harder, the giant stirred. "Go away, mother," Skyrmir mumbled in his sleep, still amid a dream. Thor returned to the camp and tried to sleep again. His mind was tidal with the waves of thought crashing over each other. "How strong is this giant?" he asked himself before closing his eyes.

The dawn approached, and Thor was ravenous. A crippling hunger that made him weak and desperate. He grabbed Mjolnir a third time and crawled up the giant's face onto his forehead again. The darkest cloud rolled overhead. The thunder rumbled loudly as Thor raised his hammer as high as he could. The noise woke Loki and the children as they looked on in fear. Using every reserve of strength left, he roared as he brought down his hammer, delivering one of the mightiest blows the world has ever seen.

The thunder roared and the lightning cracked. Such a blow could end any living thing. The impact was so powerful it was felt in every realm across the world. Even I couldn't believe the strength of Thor's blow. However, Skyrmir just woke up to the dawn of a new day, surprised to see Thor on his head.

"I hope you are all well-rested. Utgard Loki's castle is just over that ridge. I am, unfortunately, an outcast and not welcome there. Most consider me a runt of the mighty giants of Utgard Loki. Be careful little ones, the king and queen enjoy a game or two as entertainment. Consider it the gift you give for their hospitality. Best to keep your wits about you," Skyrmir cautioned as he left with the supplies.

Thor and the others stood there, amazed that the giant was still standing. A blow like that shocked them more than Skyrmir's size. He was mightier than Thor's most powerful blow but considered a weakling in Utgard-Loki's castle. The steps of their large companion that trembled the earth, faded into the distance of Jotunheim.

Reindeer Games

The four travellers were left hungry and in fear of Skyrmir's warning. They scrambled over the ridge and their eyes expanded in disbelief at what they saw. It was a castle so large and imposing it made even Thor look like a child in comparison.

The castle's doorways were the size of mountains, with walls as large as Asgard's. Oddly it had a weakness just above the entrance. "That Jotun wall builder must have built this place," Thor said to Loki, pointing toward the one imperfection in the perfectly built structure.

"Almost exactly where Asgard's weakness is," Loki said while suspiciously rubbing his chin.

Just as Thor raised his hand to knock on the door, the screeching and clanking of the lock could be heard by all. The door groaned as it opened slowly. The four traveller's jaws dropped as their eyes met Utgard Loki's. "Greetings, weary wanderers, how did you find us? I suppose it doesn't matter now. Come in. You look tired and hungry," The giant voice boomed vigorously. The four, hungry and tired, followed the king to the feasting hall, where they washed and prepared for a feast.

After the travellers were properly presented, each climbed up to the tabletop and sat quietly in wait. The queen sat next to Utgard Loki. She radiated a loving presence, both warm and accepting. Her appearance was foreign to Thor and Loki, but they were familiar with her aura. Each of them dismissed it as deja vu as they were gifted food and drink. Utgard Loki clapped his hands three times to bring the hall to silence while he announced his guests.

"Listen, all you great ones! We have been gifted an opportunity to test Asgard's supposed best. Loki, the cunning trickster, and Thor, the strong and manly one. As payment for their attendance at our great hall, they must complete a few simple games. The first trial is between Loki and Logi!" the king announced, booming around the hall, and sending the giants into a frenzy.

Emerging from the crowd, a being of similar stature to Loki appeared. Almost identical in appearance, Logi had red eyes and green hair. He looked hauntingly familiar to the travellers, with a few slight differences. Logi was like an obese Loki with a mouth drooling at the challenge ahead. He had three chins, and his arms were swollen with blubber.

"The first challenge is an eating contest. Each competitor will start at either end of the trough and whomever gets to the middle first wins!" Utgard Loki announced.

Loki walked towards one end of the challenge while Logi waddled to the other. The room filled with deafening silence, with the anticipation of the test. "Begin!" Utgard Loki yelled.

Loki's consumption was very impressive. The starvation during the trip made him ravenous. He was inhaling the food at an incredible rate. Only the bones were left on top of a pile of plates. As soon as he finished his last swallow, he looked up to find Logi already finished. Logi burped while the gong next to Utgard Loki rang.

"Congratulations to the competitors but we have our winner. Loki, your ability to consume is outstanding. However, Logi consumed not only the meat but the bones, plates, cutlery and half the trough. Therefore, great ones, I declare Logi is the winner!" Utgard Loki proclaimed. "It is now time for the next test. Little boy, step forward. You are tiny. I will send my wife away to collect our child."

The queen of Utgard left and only moments later, a small child-like Jotun appeared. "Thyalfi, can you race my child. She is quick but there are tales of how fast you fled Loki when he was having fun. A foot race to see who is quicker between Thyalfi and Hugi," the giant king declared.

I found it odd that the Queen hadn't returned but the games continued regardless. They both lined up, getting ready to race. Each competitor dug their feet in as they took their marks. "Hugi?" Loki thought to himself. Utgard Loki raised his hand high in the air.

"Go!" he yelled, bringing his hand down quickly to signal the runners.

Thyalfi exploded from the starting position. His feet were light and quick, like a professional boxer's hands hitting the speedball. Each footstep tapped the ground in quick succession. His arms moved back and forth, propelling him forward. His heartbeat evolved from a resounding drum boom to a rapid tap as he began gasping for air. He crossed the finish line quickly. Unfortunately, Hugi had already crossed and was waiting on his opponent.

Thyalfi looked up at Hugi, enraged and said, "again." They both walked to the start and took their positions. Utgard Loki signalled them to begin. Thyalfi roared as he burst from his clothes and took bear form. Four claws pounded heavier but faster than before. The gong rang loudly, this time before Thyalfi crossed the line.

"Ho ho ho! Boy, you can't win when you are human or bear. It isn't about being harmless. It also isn't about being threatening either. It is the ability to balance them both. Wrath is useful but only when controlled by a wise head," informed Utgard Loki.

"Again," Thyalfi said, raising his head from defeat.

The runners took their positions and the race started again. This time Thyalfi stayed light but also decisive. He matched Hugi's pace and only lost at the end. Still, the young lad could hold his head high. He has impressed every giant in the hall with his speed and the control of his wrath.

"Two failures so far. Lucky, I have saved the best for last. The mighty slayer of giants, trolls and ogres will have three separate tests. These challenges will not require your weapon, little god.

"Leave it away unless you are scared," taunted Utgard Loki.

"Scared, ha! I am Thor, the manliest and strongest of the gods. I will trounce your challenges."

Utgard Loki rolled his eyes until Thor placed his hammer down. "Let's begin!" Utgard Loki declared as the giants cheered. "Fetch the drinking horn!" He called out, smirking.

One giant, draped in seaweed, brings an unusual drinking horn from the back of the room. It was large with inscriptions of waves and pictures of boats. The rest of the Jotuns bang their fists on the table and stomp their feet, eager for entertainment. Utgard Loki raised his hand and the room fell to silence once more.

"Every warrior in here can drain this horn in one. Everybody else takes two but none are so weak and pathetic to take three," the king said to Thor handing him the drinking horn.

"I am no weakling. I am manlier than everyone in this room," Thor said before beginning his attempt. He raised the horn high as his head tilted back. The bitter brew filled his mouth and cheeks. With one significant swallow, Thor lowered the horn. Thor looked into the horn and it left a salty taste in his mouth. The ale within had barely dropped.

Utgard Loki smirked at his failure as the room was in shock. "You have failed, little god. Since you are small, I'll allow a second attempt. Surely a child's portion should prove your greatness, mighty thunder god," Utgard Loki mocked.

This time Thor filled his mouth, throat and cheeks. Each reached its capacity as the great hall of giants watched on in amazement. Another large gulp echoed around the silent room. Thor's face changed to bright red with embarrassment as Utgard Loki burst into laughter.

Thor became frustrated by his failure and raised the horn again. His throat expanded, his cheeks stretched and the amount of liquid he consumed was frightening. As he finished his final attempt, he lowered the horn, only to realise a small fraction was gone. The same giant came through the crowd to collect the horn nervously.

"Fail!" Utgard Loki declared. "Maybe not as manly as you thought, little god. Perhaps a test of strength, then. Little Röskva, could you please fetch the cat from the fireplace?"

"The cat? It is unfamiliar to me, and perhaps it would be better if someone it knows collects it," she replied sweetly.

"Ho ho ho! This is a strong little girl! Ok, little one, I'll get my wife to bring it. She seems to have more control over the animal anyway."

Suddenly the queen emerged from the crowd holding a scruffy-looking cat. Its eyes met Thor's and it began hissing aggressively at him. The queen placed the cat down, settling it with a few gentle pats. The cat curled up and returned to sleep. Thor tightened Megingjord and boldly marched toward it.

"Lift the cat, Thor. If you can raise it completely off the ground, you will have proven your strength," Utgard Loki stated.

Thor set himself up, grabbing the cat in the middle. Thor pulled and heaved. He pushed and wrestled the cat. It was a great struggle even for Thor but he eventually raised it to his full stretch. Grinding his teeth in the effort, then roaring in victory. The room remained quiet. Everyone in the hall could hear the faint sounds of rumbles in the distance as Frigg feared for her boy.

"Fail!" Utgard Loki's voice boomed. Thor looked around and noticed that one paw remained firmly on the floor. The cat's eyes opened and its head turned towards Thor. Suddenly, the Queen stroked the cat's head to calm it. She took it from Thor quickly and removed it from the room.

"Strong? You don't know the meaning of the word Thor. You can't even lift a little cat. I was going to fight you as part of the last challenge but now I'll give you an opponent more equal to your level. Fetch Elle!" Utgard Loki called out.

Just then, an elderly lady appeared from the crowd. She was wrinkled and weary. Her hunched back looked like she was carrying a sack filled with the sands of time. Thor was insulted but also realised he hadn't been successful in any of the previous challenges.

"This is Elle. She is harsh but forgiving. She has taught me a lot over the years and is very experienced in wearing down any opponent she crosses. She will be your wrestling opponent. Ready, Begin!"

They grappled and twisted, only breaking to regroup. Thor was surprised by the old lady's strength but didn't hold back. He used every ounce of his own strength and his impressive fighting prowess. Even though Thor's strength was great, Elle remained unmoved.

She started fighting back, causing Thor to dig deeper but sadly to no avail. No matter how hard he struggled back, one delicate touch by Elle was all it took. Thor dropped to his knees and, in doing so, failed the challenge.

Utgard Loki smiled. I was proud of my boy's accomplishments. I would never tell him the truth of it but even in his defeats, he was a champion in my eye. I only hoped that he'd learn humility in his failure but as the shame set in, everyone returned to their seats. The entire hall respected Thor and the others. Everyone just returned to eating and drinking quietly as the travellers sulked.

"Tomorrow, I will escort you to the edge of my kingdom. Take more than you need, travellers and perhaps I can teach you something more valuable than gold."

He Knows When You're Awake

The next day came, and the four travellers headed back to Asgard. Utgard Loki guided them from the castle to the outer limits of the kingdom's boundary. Loki carried more food and supplies than any other. He was like a greedy child trying to claim every present under the tree. Thyalfi and Röskva strolled quietly behind Thor and Utgard Loki. They travelled a great distance from the castle to reach the kingdom's edge.

"Now we are far away from my castle. I can now reveal to you some of the truth. You have been deceived, little ones. Loki, you thought you were racing a greedy giant but all wasn't as it appeared. Logi was a wildfire and everyone knows that fire consumes all. Little boy, you thought you were racing a child. It was another illusion. You were racing my thought and no matter how fast you are, you cannot outrun a thought," Utgard Loki revealed.

Thor clenched his teeth angrily. "And what about my tests?" Thor grumbled as his grip tightened on the shaft of Mjolnir.

"Ho ho ho! Your tests were the best, mighty Thor. You think your drinking ability makes you manly, yet you couldn't drain a horn. Well, that horn you drank from was connected to the sea. Your three impressive gulps created the ocean's tides in Midgard. If you had taken another drink, there would have been no oceans, and the marine life would have also ended as a result.".

The dark clouds rolled in overhead as Thor's rage grew. "And the cat?" Thor grumbled.

"Ho ho ho! The cat was not my idea, but it was genius. The cat wasn't a cat at all. It was Jormungandr. It was impressive that you lifted it but Röskva showed more strength leaving it alone. Only a fool must prove how great and strong they are."

Thor's face became white as his eyes turned a darker shade of red. "You bastard! What about the old lady!" Thor roared while he held Mjolnir free from his belt.

"Ho ho ho! The old lady has taught me much over the years. Elle is old age and wrestling with her, no matter her abilities and skill; she defeats everyone down the track. I was Skyrmir too.

Whenever you tried to wake me with a blow of your hammer, my queen placed a mountain where my head appeared. Your final blow would have claimed my life but instead made the biggest crack in the earth. What was once a mountain now in its place is a grand canyon, The Grand Canyon. You will never find my castle again. I will make sure of it."

Thor roared as the lightning flashed. He raised his hammer, preparing to deliver a world-ending blow. I realised he hadn't been humbled and, in an instant, Utgard Loki vanished. They turned back and realised the castle was no longer there either.

"Well, I'm impressed," said Loki stuffing his face.

"Let's go home. Maybe Odin knows something," Thor mumbled.

The journey back was long and silent as each of them reflected on the lessons delivered in Utgard Loki's castle.

Now it's time to reveal the absolute truth to you, good host. I was Utgard Loki. When I was Skyrmir, it was Frigg that protected me from death. My beloved saved me by moving large mountains to stop our son from ending my life.

I gave Thyalfi and Röskva their gifts but in the castle, they became Thor's children. Thyalfi learned to control his wrath, becoming Modi while racing my raven Huginn. The sweet little Röskva had the gift of strength and became Thrudr when she restrained her application of it. As a father myself, I thought giving Thor a daughter would soften him and give him a more caring side.

Daughters make fathers more cunning in their approach to battles.

Loki's test was about his dual nature. It was Geri and Freki at either end of the trough. The challenge was between his hunger to be accepted amongst the Aesir and his greed for power. Sadly, it was his greedy side, empowered magically from Mimir's ring, that won the test. Such is the nature of every person. I hope your priority is need over your greed, good host—the wise know which is which.

Thor's tests were tests of inner strength, good host. Njörd's horn was full of Aegir's ale and it takes more inner strength to refuse a drink offered to you. Relying on your consumption of alcohol to define your greatness will only leave you sick with a sore head. Regardless of your tolerance, too much will kill you.

The cat was a symbol of love. Love should never determine your greatness. Love is one of the magickal things in life but your ego should not be raised because of it. If it does, watch love turn nasty and that which you prize yourself on will be your undoing.

Elle is great if you understand the adaptability that comes with it. We can't be young forever and wrestling old age will leave you tired, poor and unaccomplished in life. Old age is the gift of survival. Share knowledge, stories and wisdom to help the young develop. That's always been my goal in this life and even in the challenges yet to come.

It's the Season for Love and Understanding

Good host, do you recall Freyr's disappointment at my naming a successor. He left the table and my hall displeased at my choice. He wandered angrily to my throne room and the curiosity of Hlidskjalf caught his eyes and ensnared his mind. The power of my high throne allows the reason to see what love desires, and an untamed heart can lead you far away from what you think you need.

While I guided Thor, Loki, and the children to the illusion of Utgard Loki's castle, Freyr had an internal battle. The battle between his head and heart. Freyr's head thought he was a great ruler, but his heart wanted more. He paced back and forth in front of my throne, contemplating the most challenging decision one must face. "One shot couldn't hurt, could it," he asked himself.

The power of my throne is the ability to observe what you desire most in the world. After I had my lady's heart and her companionship, I gained visions of peace in a world full of conflict. It was the power of hope. Despite the chaos the world provides, there are moments of serenity. The wisdom gained in despair is the appreciation of times of peace.

Freyr's problem was he had it all. A kingdom, a great weapon, the ability to dance with any foe and win. The problem with finding love after you have everything is you will always question, *what happens when it is all gone? Will they remain, or is their love only attached to what you have?*

Love is one of the magickal things that still remain in this cold world. A noble heart can't remain alone. It will long for intimacy and support. It is willing to give its all for love, but sadly, the intent is never appreciated by most. It doesn't matter about status; it doesn't matter about the reputation of a good man or his weapon. Love requires mutual giving and receiving so that all goes well.

This tale provides a lesson you may choose to take or disregard, good host. Either way, it is still essential, I will tell it. Needless to say, curiosity got the better of Lord Cernunnos of Alfheim. He hesitantly sat up on Hlidskjalf and placed his arms on the rests.

Suddenly, a rush of power surged through his entire body. His heart pounded hard, and he held his breath as his mind travelled throughout the lands—such a rush for an unfocused mind. Flashes of light and images in abundance as the realms were scouted.

First was the blistering heat in Muspelheim, diving deep into the Volcano called Emi koussi. Deep beneath the Sahara, my brother, Farbauti, delivered the final strike on his flaming sword. He became Surtr and will wait for the perfect time to burn everything.

From there, his vision flashed to Midgard, Svartalfheim and even his kingdom Alfheim before finally reaching Jotunheim. His gaze scanned every land, forest, and cave system in the realms until his eyes became focused.

A sight of a beauty unlike any other, she was bathing in a hot spring high above Midgard. Her sunkissed skin glistened every time the light pierced through the dense clouds. Freyr found himself bewitched by every curve, how she moved and even the suppleness of her beautiful lips. He found himself lost in the moment when his eyes found the giantess Gerðr.

As his mind forgot its physical location, he reached out toward her and fell from the throne. Shaking his head to regain consciousness, he thought twice before sitting on my throne again. Tears trickled down his startled face. His mind became haunted by visions and tortured by possibilities, and Freyr retreated to Alfheim.

Months passed as he applied direct pressure on his wounded heart with duties and distractions. A busy mind can bring clarity but what the heart whispers can soon become a deafening scream. Ignorance of the heart can poison the soul. However, love can provide wisdom that can cure one's woes.

The busy times of leadership seemed to work for Freyr, but Mani's cargo never provided comfort during the night. Beauty and desire taunted him throughout his sleep. Gerðr's image slipped in and out of Freyr's mind. The taste of her lips made his mouth water and her beautiful eyes sparkled. His imagination ran wild even though she remained far out of his sight and reach. Freyr could feel the delicate touch of her warm hands while his body tossed and turned through the night. His mind created a fantasy that felt, looked and tasted real.

Aspiration, imagination and creation are only a few of the magickal wonders of the world we live in, good host. It is the ability to create your mind's desires with the power of fantasy. You are creating an experience through a vivid imagination. The heart enchants the mind further to pursue the aspirations the mind creates.

Njörd and my Frigg became concerned with their boy. He became erratic while maintaining his usual accomplished image in front of others. Sometimes a mother knows the heart and minds of her children more than others. A minor observation of behavioural change can identify a need for concern. They both came to me to ask for my wisdom and aid in their son's quest for love.

Freyr was never my biological son but I gave him much to gain his father's favour and his mother's love. I gave him his own lands to rule and he flourished on his own accord. I had his loyalty, love and respect because I never tried to be his father. He didn't need me to be. Njörd had that role. I would be there if I were required but the good relationship with his father ensured we all wanted the best for each other.

The next day a familiar character of a different size appeared in Freyr's throne room. Freyr was busy organising his fairies that he never noticed Skyrmir appear from the fireplace. "Ho ho ho, little Freyr!"

"Who are you and what brings you to my home?" Freyr asked, grabbing Sumarbrandr's handle.

"I am a humble Jotun that has been sent from the pole in the north. Word has spread all the way to my home that you are in need of something?"

"I have a kingdom to rule and a great sword to defend it. What do you presume I need?"

"Your lands are beautiful and your weapon is extraordinary but without a queen to share it with, you have no reason to defend it."

Freyr paused as his mind wandered to the source of his restless sleep. "Well, there is one in Jotunheim that I desire."

"Gerðr is lovely, Freyr and she would make you a fine queen, however..."

"How did you know her name? Speak, gift-giver from the north!".

"What I know is mine to share with whomsoever I choose, Lord Cernunnos. If I can guarantee her hand and love, the cost will leave you vulnerable. Your sword, Freyr Cernunnos. Will you gift me your sword for exchange of the heart from the one you love?"

Freyr looked at his sword but wanted the chance to prove himself worthy of the love of another. He looked me in the eye and agreed.

Handing over the sword, I delivered words of wisdom. "Love is being vulnerable good Freyr, leaving yourself open to attack and growing together as one. A partner is the best way to grow in wisdom. It isn't fairness or equality. It is simply challenging each other, so both grow together. It is doing more for the other if you can. It isn't for praise or favour, it is simply for aid. Don't allow difficulties to get in the way. Once you both have an oath to each other, honour it. Life is hard and relationships are harder but the rewards are exponential."

I left through the fireplace with the sword, never to return to Freyr's kingdom with it. I was required to give it to another but only when the time called for it.

Three days later, the two were wed and Freyr was happy again. I used my wisdom and the power of poetry to enchant Gerðr. Mystical Words to mysterious sentences and enchanting verses charmed her, making her heart flutter and her mind focus on Alfheim's king. Their love was mutual; their hearts were pure and everything was falling into place in preparation for Ragnarok.

Children Playing and Having Fun

Frigg and I held a colossal celebration to honour Freyr's marriage to his lovely lady. I timed it accurately using my throne. Everyone came from Baldur and Nanna to Gerðr's family from Jotunheim. Even Freyr's grandparents came up from the ocean's depths. Aegir and Ran were always welcome at my table. They were, after all, my in-laws.

All had a merry time while sharing stories and laughs across the table. The large doors burst open as Thor and Loki entered after the long journey home. Thrudr and Modi followed closely behind them into Valhöll. Tyr welcomed his brother Thor while I gave my share of food to Loki. Each told their versions of events while Thor focussed on his failures. Aegir and Ran became agitated and began taunting the mighty thunderer.

"You done what? With all your strength, a sleeping snake defeated you," Aegir taunted.

"If you would let me finish..." Thor protested.

"And you drank the sea trying to prove how manly you are? It seems like you are a fool to me," Ran added.

"Enough! You can't mock someone for their failures and especially before they explain the situation. In three seasons, we will be guests at your hall. Let's see if you can provide honourable hospitality," I said to reign in the barrage of useless insults.

Three months had passed when we all gathered at Aegir and Ran's hall. Deep beneath the big blue sea, within the heart of Vanaheim. Beneath the superficial waves rolling over us is where the most beneficial conversations were held. They welcomed every Aesir in, Loki included.

As the numbers increased, Aegir apologised that they wouldn't have enough ale to accommodate such a large volume of guests. Usually, they would but Thor had drained their reserves as part of his challenges.

"I'm sorry but we simply can't provide you with enough ale to be considered good hosts."

"My father is nearby, and he has an enormous kettle to brew enough ale to replenish your stores," Tyr mentioned easing Aegir's concerns.

"I'll go since I depleted your stores," Thor offered.

"I just came from there. Hymir's many-headed mother passed, I brought her back. She is beautiful again. Caution, Thor, Hymir doesn't like you much and his mother may be toxic toward you," Loki smirked.

I glared at Loki. I told him he shouldn't use that resurrection spell but he seemed to disregard my words of caution. The gods and I sat patiently in wait in Aegir's hall. Thor and Tyr travelled by goat-pulled chariot to Jotunheim. Their hooves trampled over the lands and rumbled the skies.

Frigg was the only one that stayed in Asgard while we visited Aegir and Ran. Well, at least that's what I believed. I sent my ravens to report and record my boys and their journey. Muninn would continue to monitor from a distance but my Huginn flew faster than light to notify and inform me of worries and woes.

Thor and Tyr travelled slower than usual due to the injury to one of the goat's legs. They both journeyed over the lands and up the mountains. The sun was beating down as they travelled Midgard until they reached Hymir's peak. The winds began to pick up and the temperature dropped. Every step up the steep incline became slippery and what was once solid earth now had a layer of ice and snow. Each of them wrapped up in bear-skin coats to survive the intensity of the blizzards.

Once Thor and Tyr scaled the steep landscapes, Tyr's foster mother welcomed them inside. The door creaked under its giant size and heavy thickness. The gods appeared shrunken in the home of Hymir but Tyr's foster mother was very kind and welcoming.

"Ullr, it has been some time since you have visited. What happened to your hand?"

"I go by Tyr now, mother. My hand was a small price to keep the world safe from destruction. Sorry to hasten this reunion but can we borrow the kettle?"

Thor heard a giant covered box hissing like it had a serpent's nest inside. Unable to gain visuals, he kept his distance.

"Careful there, slayer of giants. That was a gift from Verdandi and another. Even you wouldn't be able to defeat it on your own.".

Thor acknowledged the warning and turned his gaze away from the hissing. "Can we have the kettle or not?"

"It sounds like Hymir is just home now. You can ask him. Beware, the stubborn giant will not give it to you without a challenge first, Thunderer."

Hymir burst through the doors snorting and sniffing. "Where's my food, woman? Oh, you're home, Ullr. Why did you darken my house with this red-bearded kin slayer?"

"No kin of mine has ever been slain by my hand. I mean you no disrespect, Hymir. I have come to request your help in solving a mistake I made. Forgive my intrusion. Let us eat first, good host," Thor suggested.

All three sat to a large feast. The eating began and Thor's appetite was voracious. He consumed an entire bull, three boars, six lambs and nine chickens. Tyr and Hymir watched on in awe. Hymir huffed as he aggressively stood up from his chair. "You are coming fishing with me, Thor. Perhaps a whale or two might replace what you have eaten," Hymir grunted.

"Sure, I will fish with you. I mean, how difficult could it be?".

Hymir became enraged by Thor's arrogance. "Oh well, if you are so great, maybe fetching some bait from my stables may humble you.

Sifting through my prized bull's manure for grubs and worms may change your self-proclaimed greatness."

"Take my sword, Thor. It may serve you well in that place," Tyr said, handing over his holstered blade.

Without hesitation, Thor left the table in pursuit of the bait. He went through the giant doors toward the massive stables. Heading inside to escape the cold, he found it, unlike any other stables he had seen.

A labyrinth of corridors and hallways with a few milking cows scattered throughout. It was strange how dark and gloomy the stables were. There were few flickering torches around the giant cows and the air was heavy. Silence filled the emptiness of the large compound. Thor explored the area. The deeper he went, the darker it became. The sounds of threatening angry bull calls followed haunting screams in the distance. All wasn't as it appeared in this maze of a stable.

Thor tightened his iron grip on Tyrfing's handle as he proceeded deeper into the maze. It was dimly lit, and the smell of death replaced the damp scent in the air. Bones littered the halls and blood stained the walls. Despite the gruelling horrors, Thor stayed the course.

Thor peered beyond a corner, nearing the source of the screams. There was a giant bull chomping and chewing on the flesh of mortals. Bones snapped as innocents watched, whimpering while they huddled together—Thor saw a young, intelligent man amongst those in fear. The man calculated and plotted as the beast tore flesh from bone.

Thor was mighty but so too was this creature. It was Verdandi's creation. A muscle-bound beast with its power only matched with its ferocity. Muscles rippled as its red-stained horns glistened under the dull torches. It finished crunching on the bones of its last victim and turned its gaze toward the innocents. The monster had the head and hind of a bull, the torso of a giant and the hunger of a troll.

The brave young man guided its attention to allow the others to flee. The Minotaur lowered its head and scraped the ground with a hind leg. Blood and drool puddled beneath as the hero steadied his feet.

"Hey! You with the horns! Over here!" Thor shouted bravely. Suddenly, the beast stood up and roared. Thor had his back against the wall but that was his plan. "Come on, you inglorious cow!"

Hastily, the beast lowered its head. It scraped the floor with its right hoof. Exploding from its position, it ran at Thor with immense power. Its hooves pounded the ground as the muscular torso twisted, propelling it forward. Its ugly head maneuvered one of the horns towards the heart of Thor but Thor smiled. He waited for the last moment before sidestepping driving the Minotaur's attack at a brick wall.

The minotaur was stuck, struggling to get free. Grunts and roars echoed throughout the labyrinth. Thor unsheathed Tyr's sword and with one mighty slice, Thor removed the head of the beast.

The young man cheered and began thanking the mighty thunderer.

"Boy, what is your name?" Thor asked.

"Theseus, sir," the young man said nervously.

"You may take the glory, boy. Go back to your people and tell them of how you defeated the monster," Thor said, placing his hand on Theseus's shoulder.

"Lie?" Theseus asked.

"It will be worth more in the long run. I want humans to realise their own greatness through ancestors. You and your tales will inspire great triumph for generations to come. I hope one day your ancestors will follow you. My father once told me it is better to rely on the strength and courage of your heart than the gods' aid."

Thor grabbed the severed head and placed it in a bag. He followed the path back to return Tyr's sword to him. He had the bait he needed. Now came the preparation for a fishing adventure with Hymir.

Fishing for a Great Gift

"Oh, you made it back, huh. Too scary for you to go deep into the stables?" Hymir inquired, thinking Thor was a coward, fearing to delve deep enough to acquire what was needed for the challenge.

"I got some bait. Not what I expected but I should be able to hook something great. Here's your sword Tyr."

Hymir grumbled under his breath. "We set sail tomorrow before sun up. Let's see if the mighty Thor can handle the cold and dark wave fairing."

The following day was dark. The darkest it could have possibly been. The air was still like a deadman's breath. The steep mountain descent was slippery and challenging. Standing next to Hymir in Midgard was like being on the wrong side of a cold shoulder. Hymir dragged the massive ship over midgard to the sea. It created a river.

After finally reaching the shore, the sea sprayed into Thor's eyes. The temperature was bitterly colder as the moisture in the air sat on their skin. Thor rubbed his arms, trying to generate heat and blew into his hands to get warm. Hymir stepped onto his boat easily as the ship sank a couple of metres due to his great size. Thor had to climb, scrambling on board; he grabbed an oar, eager to begin.

Both took their positions and started to row to deeper waters. Despite the size difference, Thor heaved and pulled with equal power and might as Hymir. Each pulled at a similar pace, neither willing to accept giving up. It was a battle between two greats, both physical and psychological. Where they going to row to their death? It was possible if Hymir never ceased his rowing and called, "ENOUGH!"

They were in the middle of the ocean with no land in sight. It was harsh but the waters remained calm, gently rocking the boat as Thor shivered. Hymir stood up first and grabbed his rod to cast a line. Thor gathered himself as he clutched his rod tightly. He pulled the wire back over his shoulder and roared as he launched it further into the watery abyss. Thor's cast made it a little further than Hymir's. He turned and smirked arrogantly through the shivering.

It was only moments before Hymir had snagged something big. He heaved and pulled the massive fishing pole. From beneath the surface, a giant blue whale breached. The boat swayed heavily to the side of the aquatic mammal. Thor braced on the edge while watching Hymir drag his prize onto the colossal ship. Thor reeled his line in, desperately trying to catch something.

Thor grabbed a piece of Hymir's bait and cast a line but nothing. Hymir laughed and taunted Thor as he pulled another blue whale onto the boat. Thor ground and bared his teeth out of frustration and failure. He grabbed the oars and, with one mighty pull, the boat skid across the water surface into more treacherous waters. Hymir fell backwards as the boat darted across the glassy surface.

"What are you doing? This is Jormungandr's territory, you fool!" Hymir panicked.

Thor grabbed the boat anchor and revealed to Hymir his bait. The minotaur's head sent a cold shiver up the back of Hymir as Thor placed it on the anchor. He threw it with all his strength while Hymir tried to stop him. I could see he was blinded with determination for victory. The pursuit of success pushed him closer to his final fate. I instructed Huginn to wait for the perfect time because Thor's hammer never misses its target.

Thor heaved and pulled the anchor chain over his shoulder. His feet were through the boat, standing on the sea bed. With the chain over his shoulder, he pulled with all his might turning inward to the ship. The sea became more violent as Jormungandr's head appeared on the surface. The Midgard serpent rose high above the vessel with its countless teeth dripping with venom. Hymir gasped and froze to stone as his eyes met the colossal snake.

Thor roared as the thunder rumbled and lightning clapped. Waves became tsunamis as Jormungandr screeched back at Thor. It was a world-ending battle, and it wasn't time yet. Thor leant back, preparing to launch Mjolnir. Jormungandr was exhausted fighting back from beneath the depths.

Thor let Mjolnir fly and time slowed. The hammer glided through the air, hitting every raindrop that crossed its path—slowly drifting towards Jormungandr as the giant waves appeared frozen in time. It was like death was near and every moment took an eternity to pass. It was an adrenaline rush, a heart-pounding excitement chasing your glory and willing to die for it. Quicker than most eyes could see, Huginn flew sharply, cutting the line before the hammer could connect with its target. It didn't miss. It scraped the side of Loki's son, creating an abomination.

It was a beautiful daughter, with snakes for hair and a devastating stare. It would require another hero to deal with such an intimidating gorgon. As Zeus, I'd send Perseus to deal with that monster. Her head would be a helpful tool for the challenges ahead.

As time returned to normal, Thor's expression evolved from excitement to disappointment. Jormungandr's titanic body sank beneath the waves, rocking the boat harder. The force caused Hymir to go overboard. Thor could not chase his victory beneath the waves, so he came to his senses. He pulled Hymir back onto the ship. The seawater eroded the rock that encapsulated him from Jormungandr's look.

Hymir remained paralysed by the shock of what he had experienced. He sat shaking by the two whales he caught. Thor grabbed the oars and paddled back to the shore. Thor heaved the boat and cargo across the land and up the mountain to Hymir's home.

Hymir collected himself far from the occan's waves. With no evidence of Thor's triumph, he smugly smiled at his catch. The victory for fishing went to Hymir but Thor's challenge to Jormungandr would be spoken of in lands across the world.

Time for Celebration

After returning to Hymir's home, spirits seemed to be restored from the trauma caused by the serpent beneath the waves. He dragged his whales from the deck and told his wife to summon local ogres and trolls in the surrounds. He wished to share in the spoils of his victory over the mighty thunder god.

Every Jotun nearby gathered and Hymir and his wife produced a massive feast. The meat was prepared and the tankards of ale spilled as the night continued. The room went quiet as Hymir began toasting his success.

Thor and Tyr sat quietly, despite receiving an endless bombardment of taunts and ridicules. Thor surprisingly stayed humble. He never rose to silence the fool, he never even identified Hymir's cowardice, he simply smiled through the meal. He allowed the host his glory despite the mocking of his reputation. It appeared the stone of arrogance had its magic removed. It no longer controlled Thor and he became stronger because of it.

"Hymir, congratulations on your great fishing adventures. Can we borrow your cauldron to brew ale for Aegir's hall?" Thor asked.

"Why? You lost the challenge. You do not deserve my cauldron! You weren't much of a fisher at all."

"I fished you from the water so you could enjoy your catch.".

Hymir's smug look fell from his ugly face.

"I'll tell you what, if you can break my cup, you may take my cauldron to Aegir's hall."

Thor was handed Hymir's ale cup. It was imbued with a unique aurora. It was inscribed with two familiar names. "The two that made this cup made my hammer also," Thor mumbled to himself.

"Yes, they did. It is only a cup, not as mighty as your hammer but it has some special abilities. Will you rise to the challenge?"

Thor looked him dead in the eye and turned his back on the stubborn giant. He threw it as hard as he could towards the wall. The impact with the wall was great, it felt like the house had moved. Every Jotun looked on in terror at the might of Thor. It was lucky the wall didn't support the roof. As it began to sway with such an impact.

The wall crashed down and the room remained silent. Tyr sifted through the rubble, tossing rock after rock to the side. Holding up the cup, all was revealed. Unmarked and undamaged, the room burst into laughter. Tyr walked past Thor, apologetic. "Sorry Thor, my father is pretty hard-headed."

Just then, the mighty thunderer had been given inspiration. Hymir had just filled his cup as Thor began his approach. The trolls' and ogres' laughs were seized by Thor's stern look. He stormed up to the head of the feasting table.

"What do you want, little girl?" mocked Hymir.

Thor grabbed Hymir's cup from him and poured the ale over the giant's head. He raised the cup high like a toast to the trolls and ogres. His smile was replaced by anger as he brought the cup down on Hymir's head. Gasps replaced the sound of the impact as the Jotuns watched in shock.

"Ow! My head! You broke my favourite cup. Go now and take the cauldron with you."

Thor picked up the cauldron and left with Tyr. Securing it to his chariot, he could hear the commotion inside. The trolls and ogres mocked Hymir as a fool. Tyr rushed Thor to get on their way. He knew his father wouldn't accept his defeat. They hopped on the chariot and left with haste.

Thor's goats pulled hard and strong, but their pace wasn't the best due to Tanngrisnir's leg. They went down the mountain as Hymir unveiled the gift from Loki and Verdandi. The Jotuns ran in panic, some escaped but most never. The serpent-headed creature poisoned the guests with its deadly venom. Once the toxins spread throughout the guests' blood, the screams of panic were replaced by choking and gargling. Choking on their last breath, the Jotuns' life ended and the Hydra began its pursuit of the gods. Its colossal size slithered down the mountain with a multitude of hisses echoing over the lands. Each head of this monster snapped at the next. Its venom was so toxic that nature itself could not escape its foul effects. Trees withered, and animals fell, never to rise again. It was a horror that only someone as twisted as Loki could concoct.

Thor and Tyr reached a swamp at the base of the mountain. The goats became stuck in the thick mud beneath the marshes. The heroic gods could hear the hissing approach. Tyr drew his sword and Thor his hammer. They were both ready to fight but unprepared to face the monster that followed.

Breaking through the dead trees, the heroes couldn't believe their eyes. It had three monstrous snakeheads sharing a single body and tail. This hydra moved into position, preparing itself for an attack. The heads spat venom, which Thor and Tyr managed to avoid. Even a touch would sizzle and erode their skin.

Tyr bravely sliced each head off after Thor clubbed them with Mjolnir. The blood that dripped from the neck scorched and charred the earth, and the heroes thought themselves victorious. Unfortunately, it wasn't that simple. The body and tail convulsed, which ended the premature celebration. Each neck spewed out two heads where one used to be.

Tyr became enraged. He wildly sliced each head repeatedly. Few heads turned to many, and the monster was far more intimidating than when it was released. It wasn't long before the heroes faced the nine hundred-headed monster that was once Tyr's grandmother.

"Tyr! I have an idea! Slice every head you can, and when I give, the signal, go for the heart!"

Tyr tightened his grip. Unleashing his bear inside, he attacked with a courageous roar. As each head fell, Thor summoned lightning from above to sear the wounds. That hindered the creature's ability to regenerate. It was just enough time to allow Tyr to deliver the fatal injury to its heart.

Tyr and Thor returned to Aegir's hall with the cauldron. We had an in-depth discussion on how to proceed regarding Verdandi. There was only one option available, I would have to learn the Runes.

Three Wise Men

Much discussion was had in the halls of Aegir as Hymir's ale was savoured. After deep thought and debate about the present threat of Verdandi, I had to organise my affairs before seeking the wisdom of the Runes. It would be a long perilous journey but the wisdom that comes with the runes would be the most beneficial in the times to come.

All gods returned to Asgard, and I went to see my wife, Frigg. The discussion was intense. My heart ached as I delivered my final plans. I knew we'd never be the same again. She refused to believe it was the only option. She offered anything and everything to sway my mind from purpose. I smiled at her and gently wiped a single golden tear that trickled down her warm cheek.

"I don't want to go to my death, but I need to. Not for me but our children, Frigg. Next time we meet, my beloved, I will be a stranger. Perhaps I'll be nicer. Calleigh, don't you know you're everything, and I swear on Gungnir I'll come home."

Tears turned from trickles to streams down her face as her heart broke. It was my burden but never my intention to break her heart. What kind of father would I be if I can't make peace with Verdandi. She continues to test me and my family. Loki has also become a more internal threat to my kin. He seeks to harm Thor, challenge Tyr, and his jealousy could drive him to kill Baldur. They can fight their own battles but something big was coming to Asgard. And only I can bring about its end.

It was the hardest thing I had ever done, turning my back on my wife. She wanted me to stay, happy with who I was but I needed to become more. This was an unavoidable fate that every person of wisdom makes at least once. As I walked away from my wife, the door shut behind me.

I never looked back. It would have only made it harder to do what needed to be done.

My next destination was Thor. He would attempt to save me but that was not required. To lead you must understand the path of a servant. To rule, you must observe other rulers. To be the god the world needs, you must observe another in your place.

"Listen, son. Face the monster I become. It will be greater than anything you have faced before. Your glory will echo through time but after my death, it'll be a time of peace. The time for heroes will be over, agriculture may be the way to keep the old ways alive in the times to come."

"But father, I can defeat anything Verdandi throws at us. Why don't we kill her and be done with it?" Thor suggested foolishly.

"I know you could, my boy, but this is a task for me and me alone. You can't kill the present unless you bury the memories of the past. Some will see you as cruel, and others will fear you but if you have influenced enough people, your memory will live on through them. It will be your journey to destroy the monstrous image others create of me. Seek out the mortal known as Perseus. He will give you what you need. The boy Theseus will also aid you in defeating the monster I will become. Good journey, my son. May your glory be swift, and your health be all the wealth you need."

The next stop was the heir of Asgard. Baldur was raising his boy, Forsetti. They played innocently together, bringing me peace while dealing with my internal struggles.

The world is a magickal place, good host. Some find it in the face of their children. Some find it in their lover's eyes. I see it in the future, with purpose on my mind. Look to the past to inspire a future. Genetic's history is tomorrow's mystery. The mind's imagination is only limited by reality's creation. Kinship is key, so aspire to be free. Love will last longer than you and me.

"Baldur, have you got a moment?"

"Yes, father but I bet you already knew I would."

"You won't see me again, boy. Not like this anyway and I must apologise."

"For what, Allfather?"

"I'm afraid I need to allow another to take something from you. I will use what you leave behind but when I return it and all is said and done, you will become the leader you are supposed to be."

"Ok," Baldur said, puzzled by the words of my voice.

I turned to Forsetti, crouching down to his ear. "Remember, boy. Listen to the words on the lips. Understand their past struggles to identify the superficial reasoning behind their actions. The truth is rarely simple but only the ignorant remain blind to it."

I left towards Himinbjörg. My journey to Jotunheim would be hard and I would need aid. Two others would accompany me on my journey to face Verdandi. The journey to my destiny needed aid but the fight was mine to face alone. Heimdall and Honir would travel the world to inspire peace in Midgard.

Three gods left under the guise of wise men. We travelled east and Thor went on his journey to cross paths with Theseus and discover Perseus. The land of Greece was full of wise philosophers and mighty warriors and Thor required the best for the task up ahead.

All could feel my wife's sorrows and woes in the land. The world was cold and snow fell like the salt of wisdom. It fell gently, drifting down depressingly only to feel the earth's warm embrace. It was blissful. Not one piece of snow was disturbed and white as far as my eye could see. Despite the cold, it was beautiful, innocent and peaceful.

Our first stop led us deep into the heart of the dark forest in Russia. Twisted branches were hauntingly woven into shadowy monsters that steal most men's courage. We had to find the one known as Baba Yaga. Her crooked cabin walked amongst the trees in search of her victims.

The young, the brave and the innocent were the sources of her hunger. She would tear them apart, devouring them after they were stewed.

Baba Yaga was Urd, my mother, and time had turned her monstrous too. Finding her log cabin wasn't our most significant challenge; it was destroying her. The past can be twisted by others just like she was. History can be viewed and perceived in many different ways, but judgement and misunderstanding are toxic to the truth. Urd was supposed to inspire us and teach us that no matter how bad the present is, we have come a long way since the past. Life may get hard, but do you think they didn't have the same struggles in the past with less favourable conditions.

The door to the cabin crept open, and the dim light of a candle in the corner flickered. All three of us entered with weapons drawn. The smell of death was in the air as the floors creaked with every step. The minimal amount of light that the candle gave began to fade. Only a bubbling cauldron remained in view. The smell was foul as children's body parts floated and stewed inside the pot.

Suddenly, the floor began to lift, as the cabin stood up. The fight that was pending just got more complicated. The house rocked side to side as it strolled through the dark forest. Heimdall helped Honir gain his footing as I steadied myself with Gungnir. "Baba Yaga! Show yourself! Unless you are scared to step into the light!".

The room remained dead quiet, with only the cabin's footsteps filling the air. A witch's cackle filled the room. The sound stopped and, in its place, bones cracked, muscles stretched and the old lady groaned. One thud of a heavy foot followed the other that dragged behind.

Slowly, she emerged from the shadows. Her eyes remained covered in darkness as her hideous form was revealed. She was tall but hunched over. Her arms were a little more than bones. She had three teeth in her mouth, two on top and one on the bottom. All had a yellow tinge, that revealed her horrible need for the cauldron pot. She boiled the tender meat of the young so she could make the flesh softer to devour.

Heimdall tried to reason with her to give us time to attack. Sadly, it didn't work. She rushed in, throwing him across the cabin. She turned her attention towards Honir. He clutched and grabbed his bag as she approached. Stumbling backwards, he found what he was looking for. Falling back, he pulled out a mirror. Baba Yaga was shocked when she laid her eyes on her ghastly form. She searched her reflection with her hand, trying to discover the beauty she once had. Taking the only chance I would get, I ran Gungnir through her heart.

She fell, my mother, my teacher, was dying and it was by my hand. As she took her last monstrous breath, the cabin returned to normality. A blinding bright light flashed, Illuminating the space where my mother lay. Regaining our vision, a familiar sound was heard. A raven's call and black feathers stood in front of us. My mother had been with me all this time. She was Muninn, and just like that, she flew off.

Part one of the journey was now complete. Now we were off to Bethlehem to visit a small boy that would change the world forever.

Away in a Manger

The journey was made harder as the winter's winds washed over the lands with ice and snow. It delivered a deathly chill that would wrap its fingers around the souls of weaker men. The footsteps were heavy and slow as we pushed through the rising snow. First, it was knee-deep but before long, we used arms and staffs to plough through. If we weren't gods, we would have perished.

As we continued our travels, cold became hot, and blizzards evolved into sandstorms. Each step collapsed under our feet, making sure footing on steady ground a myth. The path we took, like most, was not guaranteed. Our steps were unsure and unsteady, but we moved toward the future regardless.

We worked our way west toward a small town called Nazareth. After making it to that town, we would head ten kilometres northwest toward an old wooden stable in Bethlehem. It was summer there and the stars were clear in the skies above. Each ember reminded me that even gods are small in the vastness of Gunungagap.

It took three knocks on the stable door and a man called Joseph answered. He welcomed us in, thinking us no more than weary, wise travellers. We informed him of knowledge of astrology and constellations, and we were thought of as kings and mages. Joseph and Mary hosted us in a way that showed them as noble people. Stories were shared with wisdom and awe, but our purpose did not solely lay with them.

These people never had much but at least they had shelter. The size of a house does not make a home. A home needs heart. A home requires observing threats from the outer and inner. A home demands motherly care. A home is essential for kinship to thrive.

They took us towards a child in the back of the stables. He was a small child that would be the test of man. His name was Jesus Christ and we had to guide him despite the ones that would use his name for terrible things.

Suddenly, another knock at the door. It was a shepherd with a sinister smile. I could see beyond his disguise even though the others couldn't. It was Loki, and I knew his desire and what he wished to unleash on the world. Why did I allow it, you ask? Well, it was doomed to fail in the long run. All the gods would have to endure the hard times to come. It would be the power of the people that would bring a god to his knees.

The first gift to the boy was from Heimdall, the golden toothed. The small boy was in awe of this wise man. His words were far more valuable than any riches. "Remember your responsibility. It is to keep the traditions going. Honour your mother and father. Appreciate their sacrifices in their lives to benefit yours," Heimdall said, inspiring Jesus to honour them and the old ways.

The second gift was mine to give to Jesus; It was common sense. "Listen well, boy. A shepherd can lead sheep but that doesn't make him a leader among men. People are not simple creatures, and leadership is earned through every decision and action you take. Help who you can but in the end, people must save themselves. When the time comes, you'll know your presence is not always a gift to others. Never trust the one pretending to be the god of sheep. You are no lamb unless you are intended for the slaughter."

Haunting as the words were, I could tell it shook his foundations. He was a young boy, but it would resonate in his heart and mind for the rest of his life.

Honir stepped forward as I stepped back. He pulled a mirror from his bag. It was the mirror he had used to defeat Urd. He began to explain its cryptic meaning. "We rarely have an outward perspective of what and how we appear to others. When considering honour, we must consider the implications of our words and actions. If we can help, do we? Most people can help themselves if given no other option. Always reflect on everything you do. It is wise to assess your actions and words before you execute them. Talk when it's important and act only when it is needed."

We left the boy to his family and Loki as there was one more to face before my journey would end. Loki offered gold, frankincense and myrrh in exchange of loyalty and influence over the boy. His desire was to become the only God. Loki would need another to mould into his image and spread word of Loki's veneration. Unfortunately for Loki, my words of warning about shepherds hit true and the boy refused wealth and things of great value.

I told Heimdall and Honir that this last part of the journey was mine and mine alone. They had their roles to complete to ensure the longevity of paganism. Heimdall would live with Gríðr in Iceland. There he would lurk amongst men influencing things behind the scenes as much as possible. Honir would return to Asgard as an advisor to Baldur.

Over the ages, Heimdall and Gríðr would provide shelter to gods when required. As each retreated from Asgard's glory, they would exist under many names. Some were known as priests, politicians, wolves, Bogarts and even the Yule lads over the millennia to come. I'd be gone but this was after Loki had the power to exile.

My companions left as I made my way to Mimir's well. There I would confront Verdandi for a final time. In an attempt at peace, and my fate would leave me changed forever. This would be a time for men and women to take as much as they could. It was in the Midgard's hands to ensure the world's survival. Imagination will be the key to keep the gods alive.

Each step in the sand disappeared, covering my tracks. There was no way to find my way back. I was alone on this path and I could barely make out what was ahead. Into the unknown, I walked without fear. My thoughts of the ones I love would guide me to the place I hadn't visited for some time.

The ash tree stood magnificently outside my uncles well. It stood firm in a place where the lands had withered and darkness defeated the light. It was a place I learned, a place I drank, and a place I surpassed my wise teacher. This is where I'd face Verdandi one last time. This is where I would learn the magic of the Runes.

Tanzanite

Meanwhile, far from me, Thor travelled Midgard in search of a hero. Not just any hero but Ryujin's daughter's slayer called Perseus. His journey led him to Greece, where he met an old friend.

Theseus was living like a great king, a noble leader of the people. He was granted kingship after claiming the glory of defeating the minotaur. As soon as Thor was in his company, Theseus knew he had to return a gift for all Thor granted him. An honourable person is never so elevated that they cannot return a gift for a gift. Nobility is honoured by your actions, not another's.

King Theseus packed what supplies he could and left with Thor to travel the world. Perseus' legend had reached his kingdom. Theseus knew where they could find a clue to his whereabouts. He was a slayer of a great monster that plagued the world of mortal men.

"There is a tavern in the deepest and darkest of forests. It is said that monsters of all kinds gather there. If a hero was trying to increase his legend, you should start there," Theseus informed Thor.

"What great triumph did this hero accomplish, good Theseus?"

"Perseus accomplished what no other could, he defeated Medusa. Medusa's origin is mysterious at best. Some blame Poseidon, others blame Cetus. Either way, she tortured men and heroes from all lands. It is said her beauty was so enchanting that heroes would be ensnared by her eyes. Frozen like statues, they would become her trophies. If you were lucky enough to avoid her eyes and instead ran your fingers through her hair you would be poisoned with venom. It was like her hair contained a serpent's nest each with the deadliest venom known to man."

"Sounds like the victory of a wise man," Thor said as he recalled his fishing trip.

"Legend says he was the son of Zeus, your father is a king of gods."

"My father puts many on their path to glory. All claim they are descended from him."

Their journey took them far and wide, following legends, myths, and folklore that heroes left behind. Stories turned to whispers as the travellers became tired. The quieter people became, hinted they were close to the truth. The people were filled with fear and at times a person's silence speaks volumes. Telling the truth may result in consequences but the fear will leave you alone in the dark.

After months of questions, even the wildlife became quiet. The rain poured on the edge of Svartalfheim. Escaping the downpour, Thor and Theseus entered the dark forest realm. They found shelter at an unusual bar in the dark wilderness. The sounds of grunts and roars echoed throughout the land. They approached cautiously in an attempt to avoid an altercation with whatever Jotun existed there.

"You can't use your name, Thor. You'll incite a riot. I don't feel like a fight. You can be called Heracles and no one will know who you are," Theseus warned.

"Heracles?" Thor said puzzled.

"Yes, it means hero, warrior and glory, son of Zeus."

Walking through the door, Thor noticed a worn sign above the bar. "Fjalar's inn," he mumbled to himself. He had heard the name before but could not recall the source. The roars and grunts lowered to grumbles and groans. There were beings of all backgrounds here: Jotuns and Dark elves. As Thor walked to the bar, all eyes were on him.

"Ah, fresh blood. Fjalar was my name long ago, but I go by Eitri now. What is your name, hero? I feel our paths have crossed before," the innkeeper asked.

"I'm Heracles, son of Zeus. I have no memory of you, little goblin," Thor lied, not to draw too much attention to himself.

"I am no mere goblin hero. If you think yourself too big and strong, perhaps a challenge might determine your greatness."

"I do not seek challenges anymore."

"Oh, come on, son of Zeus. I wager free drink all night that you cannot defeat my brother in an arm wrestle."

"And if I lose?"

Just then, Brokkr appeared through the crowd. Shorter than the troll, he brushed them aside with ease. Thor knew this one, due to the presentation of his weapon. He knew it was a goblin enchanted by Verdandi's magic. He was also imbued with great power from the mead of poetry. Thor was cautious of the challenge due to his failure at Utgard Loki's.

"I'll have your strength," grunted Brokkr.

"My strength? I am strong but I am not stronger than my daughter."

"Perhaps your daughter's strength, through marriage?"

"Let us discuss the terms of our arrangement outside. Far from the gaze of others."

Thor walked out the door as Brokkr followed. They proceed to discuss, in detail, the terms of their agreement. Open-ended questions that promoted the dialogue to continue for hours. Thor countered every creative question Brokkr delivered with a strong and bold reply. It was no longer a battle between creativity and strength. It became a challenge of wit and awareness.

Back and forth, it continued as the sun crept up on the horizon. The little dark elf remained distracted by the game, trying to draw Thor's rage out. Thor was no longer the arrogant god he once was; he remained reserved. I watched my son proud of the god he became.

Suddenly, a silhouette appeared in front of the rising sun. It wasn't big but it carried a bag by its hip. "That's enough, you little vampire," said the shadowy figure.

Interrupting the challenge sent Brokkr into a frenzy. His eyes turned yellow while his fangs grew. His civilised form morphed into a creature of horrors. Brokkr became a vampiric creature that would terrify most heroes. With sharpened claws, he was ready to end the shadowy figure. Brokkr launched himself at a great pace. He moved swiftly toward his prey.

The man saw this and leaned over to grab something from his bag. He moved just enough to blind Thor for a moment with the sun behind the figure's back. While Thor turned to rub his eyes, the mysterious shadowy character pulled a trophy from a previous victory from his bag. As the weapon gazed on Brokkr's charge, he began to slow. In Brokkr's place stood a monstrous statue. The inspiration of gargoyle statues for the future to come.

Thor raised his head once his vision became clear and silence fell across the thunder god. He watched the man close his bag after placing something large inside. In awe, Thor looked to where Brokkr had prepared his attack. In his place, he was frozen in time.

"Are you Heracles?"

"Who is asking?" Thor replied.

"An old man nine years ago told me I had to kill a monster and seek out Fjalar's inn. There I would find a man named Heracles and he would have a mission that would allow my glory to echo throughout the ages. My name is Perseus, slayer of Medusa, the daughter of Cetus."

Thor invited him for a drink with Theseus. This would be the start of their epic quest together—an ocean voyage in search of a land that was deceiving. An Island at the end of the world, tempting those lost at sea with a lie.

It will be the lesson I leave to the world, good host. Salvation appears as a haven but the closer you get and the deeper you go lies the monstrous truth. On the surface, there is possible kinship, but beneath the waves of thought, danger may drag you under. It will always be wiser to watch and observe from a distance.

Written in the Stars

Now that everything was to my plan, I could walk towards Mimir's well without fear. Things were in place for what was to come. Alone in my journey, I felt at ease with my decision. Life had been a constant battle between Verdandi and myself. I would not allow her to affect my children anymore. Jotuns granted great power became more threatening with each attack they attempted. It had to come to an end.

I was cold when I reached Jotunheim. The days bled into the night as my hope dwindled. Not even the stars shone through the dense clouds to light up the darkness. My time was becoming gloomy as I prepared to gain my last form of magic. This would be the magic I needed to defeat the greatest enemy to cross my path.

The last time I was at my uncle's cave, I had a game of riddles, but this time, it would be a test of will, her's against mine. There was only one way to defeat her. I can't destroy the Norn of the present, but I can sacrifice my life to be at peace with her. The only way to defeat the present is to let her destroy herself. Find peace despite the chaos, find the quiet amongst the noise and find joy in the development through struggle. You cannot control her but you can wield your most versatile weapon, your mind.

The entrance to the cave was darker than before. Not even shadows existed amongst the blackness. I blindly proceeded deeper into the cave, stumbling on loose rocks. Using Gungnir to feel ahead, the drips from the well echoed in the silence. Finally, I came to the entrance of the well. The moss on the walls illuminated the opening with Mani's glow.

"What do you want, old god? Are you eager to die?"

"Verdandi, show yourself!"

"Behind you," she whispered.

I turned to face her, noticing the single strand of thread leading to her web. She was giant with the body of a beautiful maiden and the sinister legs of a spider. Every time she scurried, the hairs on my neck would stand on end. I threw my spear toward the entrance as a gesture of peace to the immortal witch.

"I grow tired of your games, Verdandi."

"I play no games, poor Odin. You come to me for peace while one of my children lays at the bottom of the sea. Another is in Tibet while my daughter rules over those not worthy of your halls.".

"They are where they belong, Angerboda. What is the price you demand! What will it take for you to leave Asgard and Midgard alone?"

She paused to consider what torture she could conjure from the dark corners of her mind. Using her web, she grabbed my legs and dragged me to the tree outside. The one that remained the gateway to Urd's well. She wove a web around my legs and hauled me high up in the tree. Hanging from the lifeless branches, I dangled like a bauble. As the blood rushed to my head, I drifted in and out of consciousness. Hanging there helplessly holding on to life, my victory had to be endured. Mustering whatever strength I had, I yelled out.

Hastily, appearing from the darkness, my ravens, Huginn and Muninn, flapped and fluttered around the cave. They pecked and swooped at the giant spider causing her distress. The witch attempted to swat them away, but they were too strong for her alone. Their beaks drew blood as the spider Jotun became disoriented.

My vision faded in and out of clarity. One moment birds fought a monstrous spider, and the next, three maidens in a glorious battle. I knew my mother and Angerboda but the third remained a feeling in my heart. I was unsure with unclear sight, but I felt like I knew Skuld. The way she moved, her shape, even her delicate smell, filled the dampness of the cave. It was Frigg, my beloved and it warmed my heart to see her in my final moments.

My thoughts were with my love as my eyes looked toward an opening in the roof. I no longer focussed on my death. I started looking out to the world reflecting on what story I left behind. Beyond my friends or family, I wondered what I gifted to the world. Will people understand why, or will they even remember? My story is one of growth and development but is that how I'd be seen.

The battle of the Norns ended after Verdandi grabbed my mother and tore her heart from her chest. As my mother's body fell, Verdandi devoured the heart of Urd. The earth wept as the past fell from life. Darker times were ahead in the realms without Urd as guidance. Those that fail to gain wisdom from the past are doomed to repeat their mistakes. Yet the world and its inhabitants would have to endure.

My mother's death was hugely significant across the world. Everyone forgot everything. Few pagan stories survived and those that did were fragmented beyond recognition. Any complete story was destroyed and wiped from the history books. The families in Midgard continued traditions but most of their meanings were lost over time. Yet the world would have to endure.

My Frigg flew away in grief and to protect everyone else. If she died, there would be no future for anyone. No possibilities of hope or survival, she was my light on the horizon as my mind drifted across an ocean of thoughts. I knew she was aware of things that were going to happen, but I remained clueless that she was also the Norn called Skuld. As long as she lived, I had a reason to return.

Suddenly, unable to move my arms, another emerged from the darkness. Those familiar green eyes lit up the dark. Behind a sly smirk, was a twisted character. His steps were light on the approach and he grabbed my spear. "Now, what do we have here? A King of gods with his world flipped upside down? Interesting," he said, stroking his chin.

"Loki, you won't win oath brother."

"I am Loki! I have suffered! I have sacrificed! I have endured all for the glory of Asgard. And what do I get? Jokes, ridicule and treated no better than your pet. Maybe it's time for me to take matters into my own hands," Loki snarled, right before plunging my spear into my side.

"I swear, Loki, I won't forget. I swear an oath that I will return. I will find my lady and then I will come for you. For the good of Yggdrasil and all its inhabitants, I swear!"

Loki sat for nine days while I bled into the well. He took my identity, my image but he could not take my character. He tore out one of his eyes and used the milky dead one I had gifted to Mimir's well so long ago. Now he could see all. He was mighty as he was cunning, imbued with magic far more powerful than my own. Power corrupts those that use it to elevate themselves higher than others.

Verdandi gifted him more magic and power than any Jotun before. He was now older, larger and his desire for the high seat in Asgard drove him mad. Once he gained enough power from Verdandi, he continued his devious plot. He was able to destroy her now with Urd dead. Loki was able to absorb the present by devouring her heart and could manipulate time in any way he wished. He could come and go in the blink of an eye, turning sane people delusional and mad.

Loki wasn't finished with me, as if hanging between life and death wasn't enough for him. He changed my form into something hideous. My arms and legs doubled in number. They stretched longer and became more versatile in movement. My body and head merged and expanded exponentially into a hard shell-like surface.

When I woke from such torture, I found myself underwater. It was a strange sensation seeing whales the size of fish and sharks the same size as tadpoles. I felt at peace, not requiring to come up for air. My tentacles dangled below, only ever being used if something approached the surface. I became the monstrous Kraken.

That day was the dark day when Loki became the Abrahamic god and Lucifer rolled into one. My fall would pave the way for darkness to appear as light. Influencing the weak of character and the unwise with money, gold, and greed. He desired to be the hero, the judge and the executioner. Loki in his appetite for adoration helped his followers seek out and destroy any records of anything before his reign. The minds of Midgard would fall first. Then he would set his sights on Asgard.

Loki began persuading the Roman empire to enforce his cause. First, they killed Jesus, then adopted him as a saviour of wrongs. They built churches on sacred pagan sites. Loki's followers outlawed witches and magic. They demonised werewolves and land spirits to create fear amongst the people. Loki's plan was ruthlessly brilliant and perfectly executed.

With the expansion of the Roman empire into Germania, they spread Loki's religion throughout Europe. When the people's beliefs wavered, he adopted Jesus's form. Loki scared the weak of will and character into worship. His great joke on humanity allowed them to believe he worked in mysterious ways. The promise of paradise after a life of devotion is a cruel lie for anyone to make. An oath without guarantee only to realise when it's too late. He toyed and played with mortals through the years as a cruel form of his own amusement.

Over the ages, a new type of people would rise. These people were the type to judge. Even the mighty began to oppress the weak for elevation. Lies and deception became widely accepted and rewarded by others. Appearance became more important than character and the honourable ceased to care. The foolish and ignorant rose to leadership. Good or bad didn't seem to matter, all that was left was chaos.

The earth still mourns my passing. Our hearts are intertwined. I go now to rekindle her heart, so the world may have hope once more. Life is more complex than simply good versus evil. All beginnings have an end, it is the way life, good host. Everything must end, in order for new beginnings. Everything shares the same fate as Ragnarök. First, it goes cold, then it becomes harsh before everything withers and dies.

My absence was required. You appreciate something more after it is gone. I let Loki have his victory; I allowed him to win. The life of a god is a long one and the game is even more so. Wisdom is knowing your enemy's moves, even before they make them. Wisdom is the application of knowledge while anticipating its outcome. Remember good host the world is a magickal place to be and I always keep my oaths.

ABOUT THE AUTHOR

I guess it is time to talk about my beliefs. I am not the type of Pagan that follows ancient and traditional practices, but I respect those that do. I do not follow the crowd and venerate the gods over ancestors, but understand those that do. I am the type of Pagan that finds spiritual wisdom from the metaphorical representation of the gods and Jotuns. I find internal strength in Thor and his stories. I find leadership qualities and self-discovery through Odin's stories. I find stories of love through Freya's/Frigg's tales. Each of the gods holds a wisdom in their characters and descriptions that I idolise and use to create my own story. The journey to the top of the mountain isn't the end of the path but it does hold a great view.

Printed in Great Britain
by Amazon